EDENCREST, OHIO

A Collection of Short Stories

by
DIANA HANNON FORRESTER

ISBN 978-0-9988045-7-6

DEDICATION

To my Parents, William and Barbara Thomas, who allowed me to live when another choice made a whole lot more sense.

Thanks to both of them.

TABLE OF CONTENTS

EDENCREST, OHIO

AUTHOR'S NOTE

I grew up in the 1950's and 1960's. A wholesome time, on the surface. A time we can look back on with a sense that they were the good ole days. Really, they weren't any better or any worse than other old days. They are just my old days. I survived them searching for the "good life" my parents believed in.

My parents were ordinary people who believed their dreams would be fulfilled after my dad graduated from college on the GI bill. I was ten when he graduated and they dragged me with them as he took job after job looking for money enough to live well. I remember the year he got a job earning $10,000. It was a cause for celebration. A time to look to the future with a smile. Those were the good old days, weren't they. Maybe you remember them, too.

We lived in a series of small towns much like Edencrest, Ohio, which I have created from my memories. I enjoyed the small towns but hated always being the new kid in school. I'm not sure I ever got over that.

So here I am with a new bunch of stories, several about the ordinary people living in Edencrest. I enjoyed writing them. I hope you enjoy reading them.

Diana Hannon Forrester
2018

THE WAGES OF SIN
Pittsburgh -1812

Elijah Grant was a tall, brittle man with a face carved into sharp planes and angles by thirty-six years of a hard, God-fearing life on the frontier. He was born and bred American having come into the world in Baltimore just one year before the independence from Britain. His mother had died in the act of birthing him and he was raised to manhood in the care of Christian women at the Baltimore Widows and Orphans home. They made him both a patriot and a chaste man of the cloth. Yes, he was thirty-six and had never lain with a woman. Truth was women scared him, caused blood to run to his face and his tongue to tie in knots.

It was only in the pulpit that he could speak with authority to women. And there he was inspired, exhorting them to chastity and goodness like his own. He'd been in Pittsburgh just two years and had made a minor name for himself among the prosperous farmer's there. He enjoyed his solitude and opportunities for studying the Bible, while he collected money to build a Pittsburgh Widow's and Orphan's Home. It was the legacy he planned to leave to the future.

He wasn't sure how he'd ended up betrothed to Charity Putnam, but God help him he had and it was only three weeks till the wedding. The thought drove a cold hard stake of fear through his heart. He could feel it even now as he stood before his congregation of faithful Methodists, Bible raised high in the air, words of damnation spewing from his lips. He'd prepared his message carefully. It was the last one some of the congregation would hear from a man of God for a long time. The Goodman and the Jordan families were leaving in two days for the western wilderness where Indians still ruled the land and life was hard and uncertain. Even more hard and uncertain than life in Pittsburgh.

His thoughts caused him to falter and pause amongst his carefully prepared words. He could feel the hotness of his ears and the thumping of his heart as he held the pause and examined the hard-edged faces of the congregation. Charity Putnam's plow-jawed face seemed larger than the rest and he forced his eyes to move past it, where they met the marble hard stares of her two burly brothers and dead-eyed father. A shudder blew up his spine and the silence in the church was broken by the expectant shuffling of bodies waiting for his next words.

Words about the Garden of Eden, Serpents and Sin, Paradise and God's fearsome wrath but he couldn't grasp them with his mind or his tongue. Elijah's preaching was second only to his praying and in this pinch he fell back on his strength. "Let us pray for the safe passage of our friends who we will sorely miss." Heads bowed in unison and the restless shifting ceased.

~ 3 ~

"Look upon these, your faithful servants with pity, Lord. Save them from the temptations of the road, protect their souls from the heathen attacks of savages and highwaymen bent on their destruction and the plagues of illness that are the constant traveling companions of brave patriots set out to tame this American wilderness." Thoughts of Charity receded as he fell into the familiar rhythm of his prayer and he was able to include Adam, Eve, the Tree of Knowledge, God's fearful wrath, and dangers waiting to waylay the unprotected soul as a part of his prayer.

He ended with a throat-bursting "Amen" and exhausted, he slumped forward across the pulpit. Sighs of relief escaped the congregation and shuffling began again as he softly asked them to join him in the hymn, "Onward Christian Soldiers". They stumbled and croaked out the first lines. Their voices were tight with emotion. But by the end of the first verse they were singing powerfully, filling the air with good, Christian electricity.

Elijah strode to the back of the church and stood stiff and tall at the door as the people filed out. He noticed several who went to the altar and dropped coins into the building-fund basket for the Pittsburgh Widows and Orphans Home before they stepped out into the April sunshine.

"A fine sermon, Parson," Isaiah Goodman said. "Who knows when we'll have the luxury of a church with a roof again."

Elijah pumped his hand. "The Lord will be with you," he said. Isaiah nodded and left the church followed by his four spindly legged sons and weary looking wife.

"Mrs. Goodman," Elijah said with a tilt of his head. Her lips smiled but the hard planes of her face didn't move. Elijah felt his ears redden and turned to the next parishioner in line.

Charity Putnam was followed by her brothers, Chance and Billy. Charity's eyes met his with a suggestive glance and Chance grinned, poked Billy in the ribs with an elbow. Elijah's knees went weak at the thought of just sharing a table with the tight-lipped Charity and the thought of bedding her made his otherwise robust necessaries shrivel, shrink and try to hide themselves inside his body. The raw humor of her brothers as the wedding approached had begun to have the same effect.

After the church emptied, Elijah collected the coins from the Widows and Orphans basket and headed for the two-room cabin behind the church where he lived. It was built of logs with gaps solidly filled so that winter winds and cold rain were never a problem. He was going to miss the solitude when he moved to the Putnam Farm and the more luxurious surroundings Charity was accustomed to. He had nothing against luxury, but thought the Lord required a certain amount of suffering for his gifts.

Elijah counted the coins and added them to the running total he kept on a scrap of paper in his money box. Seven hundred forty-two dollars and eighty-six cents with today's addition. A tidy sum, but still short of the goal needed to build a proper home for those unfortunates like himself who needed the help of others to survive. He counted all the money again as was his practice each Sunday to be certain none was missing, and that he hadn't made a mistake in the sums. Then he folded the bills and tucked them back into their hiding place on the shelf.

As a man of God his prospects were respectable, but not grand. He supposed that, as much as anything, made him vulnerable to Samuel Putnam's proposition. Charity wasn't getting any younger, twenty-six last month, and she hadn't the looks or the wiles to snare a man on her own. Samuel had offered incentives that were hard for Elijah to walk away from. Already Samuel had given Elijah one of his finest roan mares for getting about his business across the country side. When Elijah still didn't jump at the chance to wed his daughter, Samuel had sweetened the pot with a five-hundred-dollar donation to the Widows and Orphans Home fund. Elijah's God-given mission was closer to its completion and he was certain his sacrifice would be rewarded in Heaven.

Yes, Elijah owed a debt to Samuel Putnam, but he couldn't help the fear he felt.

The Goodman's and the Jordan's departed Pittsburgh at dawn's first light on April 11, their wagons loaded with all their worldly goods. Elijah viewed their mission as God's own, and he arose early to see them off with prayers for God's mercy and speed on their journey.

They had assembled on the edge of town and were a congregation of three wagons, nineteen people, twelve horses, three cows and a dog. The six Goodman's, Mary's widowed mother and their hired man Gracious were on one wagon. The Goodman's two married children and the oldest son's baby shared one wagon and the rest of the Goodman family filled the other. Rebecca Jordan counted heads obsessively to assure that none of her family was being left behind. Children ran in excited circles around the wagons and an atmosphere of adventure was in the air.

Isaiah Goodman extended a work roughened hand to Elijah. "Thanks for seeing us off, Parson. It means a lot to the women to believe that God is on our side."

"God is always on the side of right, Isaiah, and clearing and settling this land is right. You're heading into God's own country."

Isaiah clapped him on the shoulder, ended the handshake and climbed aboard the lead wagon to sit beside his wife. They'd be traveling west and south on Braddock Road to the National Road where travel was faster, as much as three miles an hour with a team of strong horses pulling together. They were going overland to Cincinnati where they'd get a boat to carry them to the edge of the western frontier.

A corner of Elijah's heart longed to go with them. In his mind they were Adam and Eve stepping out of the Garden, Moses and his followers stepping into the wilderness and though they'd need God's help every step of the way, they were surely doing his work.

The men clicked tongues and flicked reins; the horses shouldered into their loads and the wagons creaked and groaned down the road. Hands clasped in prayer, Elijah walked behind them for the first hundred yards, then he fell to his knees and prayed until he was alone and the heavy sound of wagon wheels and the high-pitched voices of the children were lost in the morning air.

In good time he arose and walked back towards town and his own uncertain fate.

It was two weeks later that Chance and Billy Putnam interrupted Elijah's nightly prayers. They had been drinking. Elijah could hear them coming from some distance, whooping, hollering and discharging their firearms. He was kneeling on the hard boards of the church floor, praying for the courage to be a good husband to Charity. It was just three days till the wedding. He looked up from his kneeling position when they burst through the front door.

"What you doing on your knees, Parson?" Chance said. "You should be out enjoying your last days of bachelorhood."

"Yeah, enjoying the girls down at the saloon." Billy said.

Elijah hoisted himself to his feet, blood rushed to his face. He tried looking stern. "This is a house of God," he said. "You are blaspheming it with this talk."

Laughter squirted from Chance. "Blaspheming," he said. "You're a man, ain't ya?"

"A man of God," Elijah said drawing himself thin and tall. "I don't blaspheme with my mouth or with my body."

Billy swayed from side to side. "You ever laid with a woman?" he said.

Elijah didn't answer but the truth was written all over his face.

"Chance, our sister's husband-to-be is a cherry." Both men burst into guffaws.

"Can't have that," Chance said. "Can't have him ruining her wedding night by not knowing what to do. God knows she's waited long enough."

"Daddy's counting on you for some grandchildren before he dies," Billy blinked.

"We'll take you down to the saloon, introduce you to Lulu," Chance said. "She'll teach you what to do."

"Yeah," Billy said.

Elijah Grant looked from Billy to Chance. His face was burning, his necessaries were shriveled and felt like they might stay shriveled for eternity. He grabbed his Bible and ran for the cabin behind the church.

The Putnam laughter was ringing in his ears as he slammed the door behind him and dropped the bar into place. He didn't put on a light and stood quivering in the darkness.

Billy and Chance made a commotion as Elijah listened. He could hear their drunken laughter as they mounted their horses and lit off. He was saved. He unbarred the door and scanned the area. No sign of them. He'd almost be glad when the wedding was over. He'd hide behind Charity, if he had to. She wouldn't let them get away with this. He took the bottle of whiskey off his shelf and had a drink as was his custom before he retired. Then he had another, another and another. More than he could justify for medicinal purposes. Unaccustomed as he was to that much hard liqueur he fell onto his Parson's cot filled with remorse, exhausted by the Putnam's and by his unrelenting fear.

He'd forgotten to light the fire and the room was dark and cold as the devil's own heart when he wakened to the soft sounds of disturbance in the cabin. An animal must have gotten in. He sat up woozily to light a candle and see for himself. Lord, he hoped it wasn't a skunk.

Small hands pressed him back against his cot and something like the breath of angels moved across his face. He decided he must be dreaming or God had finally sent him a vision, a miracle to share with the believers of his congregation. Elijah closed his eyes and allowed a prayer to pray across his mind.

Heavenly Father, I am your humble servant.

The smell of gardenias filled the air. Elijah sank into prayer and cleared his mind as the sensations continued. He'd never had a religious experience of this magnitude before and he didn't want to miss it. The Lord was surely speaking to him.

I am Yours, Lord to mold and shape to Your holy purpose.

He felt the tugging and heard small grunts of effort as he was stripped of his clothing. The air of the cabin chilled his skin and love of God warmed his heart. It was only right to stand before God without his earthly vestments. The Lord indeed worked in mysterious ways.

My soul is naked as my body before You. Have mercy upon me, O Lord.

The gentle ministering of the hand of God continued and thrills filled his heart and every limb. He felt the presence of God in every movement upon his body. It was a power even greater than he had expected.

Show me Your purpose for my miserable life, my Father who art in Heaven.

His necessaries responded in a way that Elijah recognized and became as hard and large as an oak tree in the virgin forest of this wonderful country. Maybe he had died and gone to Heaven.

Praise be to God, All praise and honor be to Thy holy name.

Elijah was enveloped in fire and water, a weight lay heavily upon him and ecstasy filled his heart. His body bucked and swayed with the effort of his passage. Surely this was the rapture he preached to the faithful.

I am in the hands of God...world without end. Amen

Elijah croaked out the benediction, opened his eyes to behold the face of God and instead there sitting astride him was Lulu the saloon tart grinning back at him.

"You sure do talk pretty, Parson," she said. "Makes me think I'd almost be better off in church."

Elijah sprang from his cot causing Lulu to slide unceremoniously to the hard floor of his cabin where she landed with her skirts bunched about her waist and the slippery residue of his sin upon her thighs. Laughter echoed outside and Elijah saw the drunken faces of Billy and Chance Putnam pressed against the single window of his cabin, the light of the approaching dawn framing them. He grabbed Lulu by the arm and hustled her out the door, and with a single move slammed the door and slid the bar into place.

He was sober, he was repentant, he was naked and cold. He fell to the floor, clasped his hands in fervent prayer. He begged God's forgiveness for himself and his holy wrath to fall upon Lulu, Charity Putnam and every Putnam ever born. His bony knees dug into the hard planks of the floor and the sun stood high in the sky before he finished praying.

In communion with the Lord, a path had opened before him. This time God had spoken to him clear as Efraim's bell.

"Get out of town, Elijah. Take the money and run."

As night fell on the day of Elijah's enlightenment, his eyes were darting and furtive. He carried a small bundle over his shoulder as he stole to the livery, saddled the roan mare, mounted her and urged her back toward his cabin and the Methodist Church. He entered the cabin where a fire was roaring in the fireplace, and a kerosene doused torch lay upon the table. He dumped more kerosene on the floor, lit the torch and from the doorway, threw it into the center of the room.

The heat and flames flashed with a fearsome bellow. Elijah jumped the mare, fumbled for the reins and rode her out Braddock's Road like the Devil himself was giving chase. He wanted to put as much distance as possible between himself and the godless Putnam's before they discovered he was missing and not burned to a crisp inside the parson's cabin.

He bent his head to the horses back and rode her hard till the glow from the meager lights of Pittsburgh and the flames from the burning cabin were no longer visible. The mare's sides were heaving between his knees, not unlike the lusty Lulu such a short time ago. The mare needed a rest and Elijah slowed her to trot, letting her cool down from the three hours hard riding. He felt for the bundle which contained his Bible, a copy of Harvey's Meditations and a change of clothes. He had his rifle for hunting and protection. He patted his chest where the $742.86 was tucked into the inside pocket of his preaching suit and he felt free. Freer than he had ever felt in his life.

For two days Elijah ran with the feeling. He ran like a rabbit...like a deer...like a man whose immortal soul was at stake. He left the road and slept in the woods during the daylight hours and let Putnam's mare carry him through the darkness. The horse became skittish and took to pulling herself up sharply whenever she felt like it. Several times Elijah was completely unseated and each time the mare ran further and further into the woods trying to escape. Elijah slowed his pace and tried feeding the horse better with food he stole from road house stables but the beast's temperament had changed and Elijah reminded himself she was Putnam stock.

His scrap of a plan was to join the Goodman's and the Jordan's; go with them to the western frontier where he could make a new life for himself. On the day he was to have married Charity, he was just one day's ride from Columbus, Ohio. He and the mare had reached an uneasy peace and he was leading her up the side of the road, stretching out his own legs while hers took a break. He figured to catch up to the wagons in Columbus where they were to turn south and take the less well-developed route to Cincinnati through territory that was still home to bands of Shawnee Indians who hadn't moved west after

Tecumseh's defeat. It would be one the most dangerous segments of the journey west. Elijah didn't want to make it alone. He figured the Putnam's would have caught him by now, if they were after him. He began to feel safe again.

Elijah arrived at the Red Brick Tavern about fifteen miles outside of Columbus on the afternoon of the following day. He left the mare with the stable boy for a full rubdown and feedbag and went to the dining room where he ordered a meal so delicious it almost made him cry. He finished it off with two pieces of apple pie that melted in his mouth like ambrosia.

The innkeeper's daughter served him. She was fifteen and healthy looking. Robust in a coquettish sort of way and she had the same look in her eye he remembered seeing in Lulu's. He averted his eyes quickly in order to avoid the blush he expected to rise from his neck, the burning he expected to begin in his ears. Neither came.

"More pie, Sir?" she asked as he was chewing the last bite of the second piece.

Elijah didn't answer right away; his mouth was still full. Nor did he challenge the wrath of God by looking up from his plate.

"My momma and I canned the apples ourselves, sir, and I don't mind telling you they're almost gone. It's been a busy year on the road. Best we've ever had and the apples are nearly gone. Better get them while you can."

Elijah shook his head, risked a look in her direction. "But I could use some information," he said. "I'm trying to catch up to some friends of mine headed for Columbus. Goodman's and Jordan's...three wagons worth of them traveling from Pittsburgh. Have you seen them?" He wasn't preaching, he wasn't praying and still the fire didn't come to his face.

The girl put a finger to her forehead. "Wagon's don't stop here often," she said. "When would they have gone through?"

"Within the past two days," he said, meeting her eyes for the first time.

The girl smiled at him and still he didn't blush. He flung an arm over the back of his chair, leaned back, settled in like he'd seen other men do when they talked to women. It felt pretty good. "There'd have been cows, a dog and a bunch of children whooping it up. A baby boy, less than a year and two young couples on one of the wagons. A hired man named Gracious?"

"Oh, Gracious. Yes, I remember Gracious." They camped just down the road and Gracious came to buy feed for the horses. That was just last night. Gracious was a strong, good-looking man."

"Yes," Elijah said. "That's him and he has a way with the ladies."

The girl blushed and reached down to remove Elijah's dirty dishes. "Yes, he does," she said.

"I married the young couples and baptized the baby," Elijah said with a measure of pride.

"You a preacher, then?" the girl said.

The girl smiled sweetly at Elijah. "We don't get many preachers," she said. Then, "The water's hot for your bath." He nodded and allowed her to lead him to his room.

He sent his preaching suit out with the girl to be brushed and pressed. She stood suggestively, he thought, outside with the door slightly ajar waiting for him to hand the suit out. He was still in the tub when she came back into the room with the slightest knock and hung his neatly pressed suit on a nail in the wall.

"Need me to scrub your back, Parson?" the girl asked.

Elijah leaned forward in the tub while she applied a soft cloth to his back, putting her strong, young shoulders into the task. Elijah sighed, said a silent prayer of thanksgiving for his amended circumstances and later praised God for the temptations of the road.

Elijah caught up to wagons the next day. They were parked in front of a blacksmith's shop. The horses were inside. He found the Goodman's in the general store buying supplies for the next leg of their journey.

Rebecca spotted him first. One hand went to her mouth and the other to her heart.

"It's me, Rebecca," Elijah said. He reached out and touched her arm.

"What...?" she started.

Isaiah stepped forward, a worried look on his face. "I thought I was seeing a ghost," he said. "Is something wrong? What are you doing here?"

"The church burned to the ground," he said. "Struck by lightning in a thunder storm and the Putnam's decided they wanted no part of a Parson without a church." Elijah shrugged. His eyes didn't waver with the lie.

"I figured they'd take you any way they could for Charity's sake," Isaiah said.

Elijah shrugged. "Guess not," he said. "I've been riding four days to catch you before you headed south."

"We'd be proud to have you join us," Rebecca said. "Never been any church buildings where we're going."

Isaiah nodded and Elijah became part of the western trek with a minimum of questions that required lies as answers. He contributed fifty dollars of the widows and orphan's money to finance his share of the trip and the following morning the small group headed south toward Cincinnati and points west.

The trail was rough and the going was slow. Thick hardwood forests loomed at the edges of the road trying to reclaim it and the first day Isaiah gave Elijah the job of riding ahead to find fallen trees or other barriers on the road. The first day they had to clear two huge trees from the road and broke a saw in the process. When they stopped at a clearing in the evening they had traveled only eight miles. Elijah's hands were blistered from the saw and his muscles ached from the unaccustomed physical exertion.

Visions of Lulu and the innkeeper's daughter danced in his head as he fell into an uneasy slumber after a supper of hearty stew and a chug of whiskey from his medicine bottle. He dreamed of Adam and Eve in the Garden of Eden, the price of the knowledge of good and evil in a way he never had imagined it before. In the middle of the night he was awakened by Isaiah Goodman. "You're dreaming Elijah, Wake up."

"What...? What...? he said and looked up at Isaiah and Rebecca.

"You're shouting about the Garden of Eden...About God casting out sinners. . . You're spooking the animals and the children."

Elijah rose up and looked about the camp. "I feel like I've had a message from God," he said. "A vision in my sleep. I think I'm as close to God's bliss as I'm ever going to get."

"It's a dream," Rebecca said. "You probably ate too much stew for supper. Go back to sleep now." She pushed the parson back to the ground and she and Isaiah returned to their wagon shaking their heads over the poor man's plight.

The next morning Elijah rode out from the wagons toward the Scioto River. He pulled the roan up and watched the river flow south in its springtime fullness. He urged the horse down the muddy slope where her feet made sucking sounds as she lifted them for the next step. He led her around the outcroppings of rocks and she stepped gingerly. In his mind he hatched a plan for his future in the western wilderness. A plan that would set aside the teaching of the fearsome ladies at the Baltimore Widows and Orphans Home. He patted the pocket that held the money and thought of a different sort of legacy for his life.

As he sat on the Putnam mare and praised God for freeing him, a snake slithered by in the mud, scared the horse causing her to rear and throw Elijah to the ground. He struck his head on an outcropping of boulders and lay dead in the mud with his words of praise for God still hanging in the spring air.

Isaiah Goodman found him at noon. The wagoners took his death as a sign from God and ended their journey right there founding the town of Edencrest after…well after the Garden of Eden and the loss of innocence and the unfortunate plight of Elijah Grant cast out of Pittsburgh by the Putnam family and then out of the world by the Putnam mare.

Rebecca found the money in Elijah's preaching suit while she was preparing his body for burial and they used the money to buy the land and to build a road house for travelers like themselves. They called it Grant House and prominently displayed Elijah's Bible and his Harvey's Meditations as encouragement for hapless travelers looking for comfort in a hostile wilderness.

They buried Elijah on a hillcrest overlooking the river and had a beautifully carved headstone created and carried down from Columbus.

ELIJAH GRANT

1773-1812

THOU HAS BEEN IN EDEN

THE GARDEN OF GOD

Ezekiel 28:13

LOVE OF MONEY
Edencrest 1899

There is hunger of the body; there is hunger of the heart; and there is greed…
a hunger that is never satisfied.

Will Goodman watched his father at the head of the family dinner table - saw
him load his plate from heaping bowls passed by the hired girls, watched him
cover it all with gravy, watched him take his first bite, felt the collective sigh as
his mother and five brothers relaxed their shoulders, picked up their forks and
began to eat, too. Will saw greed more and more often as he watched his father.

He was twenty-two that September and had begun to feel he was a man, not
just the eldest son of John and Mary Goodman, respected citizens of Edencrest,
Ohio. Even the glances of the hired girls over the serving dishes made him
uncomfortably aware of himself…the breadth of his shoulders, the length of his
stride and the quivering loneliness of his room at night.

"Timing is everything," John Goodman said breaking the dinnertime silence.
"We get our cattle to market three weeks ahead of everybody else and it means
$2.00 more a head for us."

"It means leaving the farm in the midst of harvest, daddy," Will said. "It's
the worst time of the year to be gone to Chicago for a week."

"You're thinking small," his father said. "Nate Wheat can handle the
workers. Your mother and the boys will look after other things while we're in
the city skimming the cream off the cattle market." John looked sternly at his
son, tore off a hunk of biscuit and ran it around his plate before popping it in his
mouth. "Two dollars a head ... that won't cost us a single ear of corn or one bale
of hay. It's just smart business."

The financial lectures had become a nightly thing and were certainly the
reason behind John's insistence that Will go with him to Chicago to sell the six
hundred head of Shorthorn cattle that, even now, stood penned and ready to load
onto the train at first morning light.

"You won't forget the worsted, John," Will's mother said from the other end
of the long table. "For Jacob's new suit and a bolt of dress fabric for me." Mary
Goodman smiled but her face was drawn and tired.

"I won't forget," John said.

"Maybe a bolt of silk?" Will said. "Mother should have a silk dress like the
fine ladies wear."

John pushed his chair back from the table and stood. "No silk! We're going
to town to make money, not to squander it on foolishness like silk." The dinner

table quieted. "Pack your valise tonight, Will. There won't be time in the morning."

"Yes, daddy," Will said and lowered his eyes to his empty plate. His father strode off to his office and his mother hurried to supervise the evening kitchen clean up.

The smell of warm blood, sweat and steam rose from the slaughter house floor to the observation deck where Will stood with his father and the cattle buyer, Mr. Pipps. Will pulled a handkerchief from his pocket and clamped it over his mouth and nose to block the stench. The handkerchief helped but he could still see meat cutters who were so bathed in blood only their eyes showed white.

"We kill a steer a minute, twelve hours a day, every day," Mr. Pipps said. "The cutters say the cows are still thinking about breathing when their carcasses hit the refrigerator cars on the rail siding. It's the fastest line in Chicago." His voice was filled with pride. John Goodman nodded and Will swallowed hard behind his handkerchief.

"It's a revolutionary system," John said. "I'm glad to be part of it." It had taken two days but John had bargained a spectacular price for his Shorthorns.

Mr. Pipps clapped a reassuring hand on Will's back. "You get used to the smell."

"I don't plan to," Will answered. He'd never see a cow on the hoof again without remembering and feeling diminished by this spectacle.

"Somebody bleeds a little for every dollar earned," John said. "Learn that now, Will."

"The steers bleed a lot for the dollars you carry out of here," Mr. Pipps said and laughed at his own little joke.

Will stepped back from the railing, closed his eyes and tried to clear the vision of the bloody cutters and the procession of beef carcasses that bobbed and swayed along on the overhead conveyers.

"Your check should be ready," Mr. Pipps said. "Let's finish up our business so the two of you can get on to Chicago's more delicate pleasures."

Even back in the office, Will couldn't free himself of the smell which now seemed to cling to everything. He felt weakened by what he had seen, even desperate for an antidote if such a thing existed. His father collected his check and signed the bill of sale while Will took deep breaths and wiped his clammy forehead with his handkerchief.

"Will you be wanting to visit the Everleigh again this trip?" Mr. Pipps said to John with a sly glance at Will.

"Yes," John said. "It's always a highlight of my trip. I'm sure my son will enjoy it, too."

"I'll call and make the arrangements," Mr. Pipps said with a smile. The men shook hands and the Goodman's were soon outside boarding a horse drawn cab for the ride to the Everleigh.

John leaned back into the cab seat. "Chicago is a town where fortunes are being made. A few more shipments of Shorthorns and ours will be made as well."

"My fortune...good or bad...is in Edencrest," Will said. "With the land. I want a good wife, strong sons, and a little silk for Mama. Chicago fortunes can go hang for all I care."

John's eyes rolled, his nose and cheeks turned red. "What do you think the money's for, boy? Land! More land for more corn and hay for more cattle...for sons and wives...and God willing for grandsons." John paused for a deep breath. "Timing, Will! Stay one jump ahead of your competitors."

"More land, like Nate Wheat's land that you bought cheap?" Will's voice was loud.

"Timing? Like getting the bank to refuse him a loan after two bad crops in a row?"

"Yes, just like that!" John said. "Nate's a good man, but he fell behind and lost out."

"Now he works for you."

"Right!" John leaned back into the cab seat, his voice softened. "Nate's working the land for wages, now. That's how it goes. Never miss an opportunity to get what you want, Will. Opportunities passed are opportunities lost."

Will turned his eyes to the street and fell silent. He'd never seen so many people, so many tall buildings...some of them fifteen stories high. Horseless carriages zoomed by at amazing speeds, scattering slower traffic, scaring horses, children, and out-of-towners, like himself.

"There's more to life than we see in Edencrest," his father said.

"You're right about that," Will said. "But there's life enough for me there."

"You haven't been to the Everleigh yet," John said. "It has the finest foods, elegant surroundings and beautiful accommodating women." John studied his son for some moments. "Have you ever been with a woman, Will?"

Color climbed up Will's neck and into his cheeks. "Well no, daddy. You know what Mama would think about that."

"Your mama's a strong, hard-working woman...but men... have appetites she doesn't share." John leaned forward, looked into Will's eyes. "City women understand men better."

Will didn't say anything. He watched his father's eyes till he thought they'd burn a hole right through him and then he dropped his own eyes to his boots. "Mama says it's important to save yourself for marriage."

"Marriage matters to Edencrest women, but Chicago women are different." John Goodman's lips thinned into a greedy smile. "A man can appreciate the difference."

Will ran a finger around the stiff collar at his neck. It seemed tighter than it had been five minutes before. His face felt hot and he longed for the open fields and easy breezes of the farm. "Like the difference between owning the land and working for wages," he said.

John smiled at his son. "Exactly," he said as the carriage turned onto Dearborn Street and stopped in front of the Everleigh Club.

The Everleigh Club was the finest brothel in a city full of brothels. It was as elegant and inviting as the slaughter house had been revolting. Ada Everleigh met John and Will at the door. "So happy to see you again, Mr. Goodman," she said and escorted them to a brocaded parlor. The walls hung heavily with gilded mirrors and framed art, the floors were covered with fine oriental carpets. A piano player sat as a huge grand piano tinkling out popular music. Beautiful women and prosperous looking men sat about chatting and drinking champagne.

Ada's eyes landed on two wasp-waisted women standing near the piano. She escorted Will and his father toward the women who were deep in conversation. The taller woman placed a hand on the other's arm and their conversation stopped. Both women smiled as the men approached.

"John, Will, meet Rosalee Brentwood and Sarah Parker. They'll be your companions for dinner. . . and afterwards, if you wish. Rosalee is from Ohio, too."

"Thank you," John said. He reached for Rosalee's hand but she side-stepped and took Will's arm. "Hello," she said, looking into his eyes.

"Rosalee," Ada said. Her soft voice had a sharp edge. "I believe Mr. Goodman was about to choose you for himself."

John Goodman laughed. "Never mind," he said. "We can stay an extra day if necessary. Time enough for several choices."

"Very well," Ada said. "Are you ready for dinner or would you like to relax first?"

"It's been a long day and I'm hungry," John said.

Ada nodded. She gave Rosalee a stern look as Sarah took John's arm and escorted him toward an arched doorway covered by brocaded drapes. A butler pulled the drapes aside with a flourish and Will gasped at the splendor of the dining room. The warm glow of candlelight on linen, the rich smell of fine food, the bass hum of masculine voices enveloped him.

John smiled at his son, kissed the beautiful Sarah Parker on the lips and followed the butler toward an empty table. Will couldn't remember ever seeing his father kiss his mother and certainly not on the lips and most certainly not in public.

Rosalee tugged gently at Will's arm. "It's okay," she said. "I promise this will be the finest meal you've ever eaten and you won't have to watch your father."

Will leaned close to hear her and caught the sharp, clean smell of honeysuckle and clover. She laid a palm on his cheek. "Trust me," she said. Will's cheek burned hot as he followed her to their table. The tinkle of crystal and women's laughter quickened his pulse and curled his toes against the top of his shoes. He held Rosalee's chair and as he sat down, he touched the heat on his cheek with curious fingers.

Liveried servants poured champagne and delivered delicacies to the table. Rosalee dipped oysters in spicy sauce and fed them to Will from a silver fork. She cupped her hand under the oysters and if a bit of sauce dropped, she licked it from her own palm with a tongue that was as quick and firm as any Will had ever seen. The elegant clatter of the dining room receded as Will watched Rosalee. He noticed the flicker of candlelight rebound from her coppery hair, the reflection of silver in her deep, dark eyes, the downy hair on the lobes of her finely set ears and the polished texture of the skin in the hollows of her throat. He thought she was the softest, most beautiful woman he'd ever seen. He thought he loved her.

John Goodman intruded with an elbow on the table as he leaned toward Will...a leer on his florid face. He looked from Will to Rosalee and back to Will. "More oysters? More champagne?" he asked.

"I'm already about to bust a gut," Will said. He leaned back in his chair and undid the bottom two buttons of his vest. Rosalee shook her head no and sipped from her champagne flute.

"You only had three dozen," John said to Will.

"That's more than I ate last Christmas and this isn't even a holiday."

"Every day is a holiday when you're in Chicago. Especially when the stock yard is paying $35.00 a head for Shorthorns." John laughed.

"You may be right, Daddy, but I can't eat another bite and Rose...Rosalee's not eaten what she has."

"Fine," John said. He ran a hand up Sarah's bare arm. "There are other pleasures before us." He leveled his eyes on Rosalee and said, "Don't let the boy wear you out. I'm first in line tomorrow."

Rosalee paled at the words. "This is my last night at Everleigh," she said. Sarah shook her head and stepped forward. "No, Rosalee," she said. Will jumped from his chair and stood between Rosalee and his father.

"We'll see about that," John said to Rosalee. He smiled at Will but the smile wasn't a pleasant one. "Remember I'm next, Will."

When John and Sarah left, Rosalee stood and smoothed Will's lapel. "It's okay, Will. This really is my last night at Everleigh. I was leaving anyway."

"Are you going home to your family in Ohio?" He spoke with a hopeful tone.

"My family is gone. Mama died with influenza in '86 and my father went west in '94." Rosalee smiled prettily. "I've been on my own since then."

"Won't it be hard to leave all this grandness?" Will asked. He looked around the dining room and was surprised to find it nearly empty.

"You can only eat so many oysters, Will. The gilt and silver is just window dressing for the woman and the gambling...a way for Miss Ada to make a fortune." Her voice was wistful, "I'm ready for simpler things."

Rosalee laid a hand on Will's cheek in such a familiar way that he blushed. "Would you like to see my room?"

"I'm not sure I should." Will stammered.

"I think you should see it," she said. "Your father expects it." Rosalee took Will's hand and led him to the stairway. He had little choice but to go along.

The upstairs was as elegant as the downstairs. The hallway was at least ten feet wide with crystal chandeliers, brocade settees and art work displayed on either side. Rosalee opened a door near the end of the hall and stepped aside so Will could enter. She pointed Will to a gold settee and stepped behind a dressing screen.

The room smelled of honeysuckle and candle wax. Will sat on the settee with his hands dangling between his legs. His hands felt oversized and awkward. He moved them to his knees trying to find a spot where they seemed right. They no longer seemed to be a match for his body. Finally he sighed and leaned back into the settee wishing he could disappear.

"Tell me about your farm," Rosalee said from behind the screen.

"I love the farm," Will said. "I love the musky smell of the soil when I till, the clean way the loam crumbles in my hand. The dark chocolate look of it in the morning sun. The shades and patterns of brown in a freshly plowed field are a work of God's own art."

Will leaned forward again. "I've never seen anything to match the tender green of row after row of corn sprouting from the black dirt. There's a good feeling that comes from seeing the sides of the silo bulge and the stacks of hay in the barn loft after a harvest. It's a safe feeling, like you're home and nothing can take it from you."

When Rosalee stepped from behind the screen she wore a silk wrapper and there were tears in her eyes.

"It sounds perfect," she said. "Like the place where I grew up." She sat next to Will and said, "Please tell me more," and he did. Will talked until the candles burned low...about his farm, his brothers, his mama, and crops growing so fast you could almost see it happen.

"It is perfect, Rosalee," Will said. "It's the most perfect thing I've ever known, till now."

"Rose," she whispered. "Call me Rose."

"Rose," Will said. "Yes, Rose is better for you." And he said her name again letting it roll inside his mouth and slide off his tongue into the air.

"I'd like you to let down my hair," she said. Will nodded and pulled loose the pins that held it in place. It tumbled and fell to her shoulders where Will touched it with his fingertips. It was strong and soft and fragrant as a spring night. Will lifted it toward himself and buried his face in the softness.

"Your hair is beautiful," he said. Rose smiled. "You are beautiful," he said. Rose smiled. "Will you marry me? Go home to Ohio with me?" Rose smiled.

"I doubt your father would like that," she said.

"If we were married, he'd never dare think of laying a hand on you," Will said.

"I promise you, Will, he'll never touch me, regardless. Miss Ada knows I'm ready to leave. She'd never force me and besides I've got $3000 saved against the day I'd be able to leave. I'm as good as free of it all." She smiled at Will. "But now, I'm yours, bought and paid for tonight."

"I'm a man," Will said. "But, I won't have you that way."

"Are you very rich, Will?"

"I work hard," he said. "I know how to grow things and store them away for winter. You'd never be hungry, Rose." Will smiled. "I'm the eldest son and my daddy is _very_ rich."

Rose laughed and then tears began to roll down her cheeks. "I won't be bought ever again," she said.

"Shhhh! Shhhhh!" Will said. He pulled her into his arms. "I love you, Rose," he murmured into her hair. "We'll be married in the morning before my father suspects a thing."

"Oh, Will. Are you sure you want me for a wife? For the rest of your life, and not just tonight?"

"I've never been surer of anything in my life."

Rose smiled. "Well, if you're sure...there's a judge I know downstairs. We can do it right now."

So they were husband and wife when John Goodman saw them next morning in Miss Ada's office. Will and Rose sat side by side on a divan. Rose's hands were folded quietly in her lap, Will's arm was draped protectively around Rose's shoulders. John steamed back and forth spewing insults in short, moist bursts. His face was a red as the meat cutters on the slaughter house floor. "Gold digger!" "Opportunist!" "Whore!" he yelled at Rose. Will half stood but Rose put a hand on his knee and he sat back down.

"You!" John yelled, pointing a porky finger at his son. "You, I will disown."

Ada sat behind her desk mewing words of reconciliation. "Calm down, Mr. Goodman. These things just happen sometimes."

"This place is an abomination." John turned on Ada. "It should be burned to the ground."

"My establishment has the favor of the Mayor, the Chief of Police, the Masons and Philip D. Armour. Every one of my girls is a lady." She shrugged. "Some of them just want a change of pace after a while."

"Change of pace?" John yelled. "That's what you call this? A change of pace?"

Ada looked John Goodman in the eye and shrugged.

"What is your mother going to think about this?" John said to Will.

Will sat straighter on the divan. "Mama will be glad I've found a wife. She'll be happy I've fallen in love."

"With a whore? Your mother will never accept a whore as a daughter."

"I don't think any of us is going to use that word to Mama. It would mean explaining how we met and your part in it, wouldn't it, daddy?"

Ada nodded in agreement and they all waited for John's answer. He looked at Rose.

"Young woman," he said. "I have a bank draft for $21,000 in my pocket. It represents a year's worth of work on my land. I'll sign it over to you to do with as you please if you'll walk away from Will right now."

Will clenched his fists and started to stand up again. Once more Rose restrained him with a hand. "It's all a matter of timing, Mr. Goodman," she said. "Last night I retired from the business where I can be bought and sold. Today, I'm Will's wife. I'm going to be a good wife and the mother of his children …and of your grandchildren." Her eyes met John's. "I promise never to speak again of your insulting offer and I swear if you speak ill of me again, everyone in your dear little Edencrest will know where you found me and how. I have nothing to lose and you have everything."

John Goodman's shoulders slumped, his eyes went heavenward. "Are you going to stand for this?" he asked Will.

"I love Rose. As far as I am concerned you have no voice in the matter."

The three of them boarded the train for Edencrest later that day. Will carried a bag with two bolts of silk. One for Rose, one for his mother.

At dinner that night John ate quickly, quietly. The Goodman boys stared at Rose in awe and at Will with new respect. Mary Goodman chattered happily.

"We'll celebrate your marriage at church when the harvest's done. You'll have to meet the neighbors."

"I'd like that," Rose said.

"I never thought Will would come home from the city with a bride. And to think you're both from Ohio and had to go to Chicago to meet."

"Yes, isn't it strange?' Rose said.

Mary Goodman laughed. "I did think Will and John might forget the worsted."

"I'm sorry about that, Mama." Will said.

"Never mind," she said. "I can get it mail order and Rose is so much better."

"I should hope so," Will laughed.

"John and I only knew one another three months before we were married," Mary said. "Love is so unpredictable." Her cheeks were flushed with excitement.

"I loved Will the moment I saw him, Mrs. Goodman. And when I heard him talk about your farm and how he loved it, I knew he was the man for me."

"Rose, Rose," Mary said. "You're my daughter now. Please call me Mama."
"I'd be proud to," Rose said.

THE EVERLEIGH CLUB

ON THE ROAD
1931

It was a cruel, hungry time...a time that coaxed the extremes of good and evil from folks who otherwise would have been quite ordinary. Eve was a very ordinary woman and never would have gone on the road alone. She was timid, quiet, not one to put herself forward in a crowd. Charlie liked that about her.

Charlie was her husband. Well, he would have been if they'd had the money for a marriage license before they left Detroit, it's bitter cold winters, forty per cent unemployment and bread lines without end.

"We've got to get away from the city," Charlie said and Eve, not being one to argue, packed their meager belongings and headed for the country with him. Eve had loved Charlie in the city...but alone at night under a spring sky that sparkled with a million stars, she loved him even more. She depended on him and trusted him to keep her safe.

They walked the countryside till they learned to hop the trains, worked where they could and begged food where there was no work. Life was hard--even harder than they'd expected. As the weather warmed the roads got more crowded with others looking for food and work. Mostly single men and young people like Eve and Charlie with no jobs, no families, no roofs or responsibilities to hold them down.

"I like the trains," Charles said. "The swaying of the cars, the metal wheels clanking and screeching against the tracks. It's comforting to me." Eve thought he even liked the odd camaraderie of the hobo jungles. She hated the jungles, the hot glances of the men, the sullen stares of the bolder ones. She'd cling to Charlie's arm whenever she could.

One night after Charlie had spread out their bedroll and made a tour of the camp saying hello and asking who knew of work, a sour smelling man approached them and said to Charlie, "Two cans of beans for a half hour with your woman." The man stood over them, a toothless leer interrupting the stubble on his face.

"Go away," Charlie said and rolled over, showing the man his back.

Eve cringed and watched as another man approached them from the fire. "I've got 10 cents and a pair of spare shoes," he said. "S'pect I wouldn't need more than fifteen minutes to do my business."

A laugh went up from near the fire and more men gathered round, making crude remarks and bidding for a few minutes of Eve's time. Charlie wrapped his arms around Eve and ignored the men until the banter turned to threats.

"I ain't had a woman since Christmas and I say we take her and save our money and our shoes," a tall, thin man said. A chorus of "Yeah's" went up among the men.

Charlie stood up before the crowd got any bigger and grabbed Eve's hand. They ran, barely managing to save one knapsack full of their belongings. "A woman on the road is trouble," Charlie said. Eve cut her hair and put on Charlie's spare trousers. They'd avoided the hobo jungles through the summer...walking, hitching rides, sleeping in barns and stealing food when there was no other way.

Eve was tall, and she practiced putting her feet solidly on the ground and spreading her knees when she walked. In Charlie's clothes and with his encouragement she passed for a man. She worked where there was work to be had and earned her way. Slowly the long summer passed.

"It's time we thought about heading south," Charlie said when the leaves began to turn and apple picking was the only work they found. "Or to California. I can't stand another cold winter."

She hadn't thought Charlie would leave her, and it had all been an accident really. They were running hard to hop a B & O cattle car one evening. Skinny faces hung around the door urging them on. Charlie made the leap for the gaping door and Eve stumbled. She saw the second he hesitated...the second he thought of jumping off to come back for her. She saw his decision in the set of his shoulders as he half-waved while ropy arms pulled him inside the car and left her alone brushing cinders from her palms.

And suddenly in Eve's life it was too late. Too late to insist she carry her own share of the coins they'd earned picking apples three days straight, too late to refuse the sex she suspected had caused a baby to take root inside her, too late for anything but finding Charlie again.

She could have made it south on her own but she was frightened and she spent too many weeks looking for Charlie among the hollow-eyed men in the hobo jungles. Filthy, dank places that made her nose twitch and her skin crawl. A chill tinged the air when the sun went down and the night shadows fell harder and longer before she gave up looking for him. Her belly had started to round and she could feel the first tentative flutters of life inside herself. The fact that she was a woman was harder to hide

She pitched her voice lower, she walked with a swagger but there was always one who'd eye her and see her for what she was. She was afraid, but she was determined to get south before the winter came. For Charlie's child, if not for herself. She'd never felt so alone or so vulnerable as she slipped past freight yard guards looking for an empty car.

When she found one, she hid herself in the darkest corner, snuggled into the filthy straw for warmth. The guards shined their lights into the car before the train started rolling. She didn't move and they didn't see her. She felt safe. . . lucky to be on her way. The clackety-clack of the wheels hadn't reached their peak when three men jumped on the car, her car.

They were laughing and one of them pulled a bottle from his back pocket when they were all aboard. She shrank into the straw, hoping for a miracle. The men passed the bottle around and the sharp smell of alcohol caused her stomach to lurch.

"Check the car," the man with the bottle said.

"Think there's a guard on here?" Another laughed.

"Just check it," he said. "I don't want to get thrown off on a trestle."

So the men had walked the car zigzagging and kicking the straw.

"Hello, what's this?" the man who found her said. He pulled her to her feet and brushed the straw off her head. "God is still in heaven," he laughed. "I think it's a woman."

Eve tried to push him away, she yelled but it came out high pitched and female, as he ripped open her shirt and revealed her breasts. "By god, it is a woman," the man said. "Look at them knockers."

Eve turned from him and tried to cover her breasts. "Please," she said. "No. Please? I'm pregnant."

"And the damage is already done." The man laughed.

"Please. . .," Eve cried and let her knees go limp. She fell to the floor of the car and the man let go of her arm.

"I'm first," the tallest man said. He was undoing his belt as he spoke.

"Why should you be first," another said.

"I found her," said the third.

Eve scrambled for the open door on hands and knees but the tallest man grabbed her. "No you don't," he said as he lifted her to her feet again. "The train's going too fast."

"Yeah," one said. "Better to take your chances with us."

Eve's eyes darted like an animal, looking for an escape. "I'd rather die," she said.

"Don't want you to die, honey. We just want a little party."

Eve shook her head, tried to pull free. The train's whistle blew three loud bleats and lights of a small town threw shadows into the car for an instant. Eve listened for the sound of the brakes, but the train just slowed, then barreled back into darkness.

"I've got it," the tall man said when the town was passed. "We'll draw straws. Longest goes first."

"Mine's the longest, getting longer by the minute," another said.

"The straws, Tom." The men laughed and agreed to drawing straws.

The one called Tom held the straws and the others drew. The winner pulled Eve into the darkness and pushed her to the floor. He jerked off Charlie's trousers while she kicked and screamed.

"Need any help?" one of the waiting men asked.

"Naw," the man leaning over her said. He was breathing hard from the struggle and Eve felt one moment of satisfaction before the splitting pain of forced entry hit.

The men blended together for Eve and the pain was the only way she could tell where they ended and she began. The click of the wheels on the track, the train's whistle, the occasional lights of another small town flashing by and the pain told Eve she was surviving as the men used her till they were done. Finally they left her alone.

She tried to move but her muscles felt like oatmeal, wouldn't respond. She could feel the men's sticky residue on her thighs and their bitter smell seemed like her own. She could see them huddled together at the other end of the car. They were passing the bottle and she listened with all her strength as they spoke in the confidential tone of men who have shared either great or horrible things.

"What're we gonna do now?" one said.

"Kill her?"

"Naw, let's toss her off at the next town. She weren't bad to us."

They nodded in agreement and passed the bottle again. Eve thought death might be the better choice, but she heard the train's whistle before they had time to change their minds.

Mikey Wheat was eight years old and on his way to Jordan's General Store with a wire basket half full of his mother's fresh eggs. It was his job every morning on his way to school to drop off the extra eggs and pick up the money from yesterday's eggs. It was a big responsibility for a little boy, but he was equal to it. He was scuffing his toes into the dry dirt of the road and had just crossed the railroad track when he heard the moan. It sounded like a ghost which were much on his mind as Miss McCall was reading *The Legend of Sleepy Hollow* to her students as Halloween approached.

Mikey stopped, listened and thought of throwing the egg basket and running from the sound, but the eggs were valuable and he was eight, not a baby any more. He saw the dry weeds rustling ten feet from the road. Carefully he set the egg basket down and edged his way toward the moaning sound.

It wasn't a ghost at all, but a woman and she was naked, fat in the belly. One arm was bent under her head at an odd angle. Mikey stepped back but was drawn forward again by the sight of her pink nipples and the patch of dark hair between her legs. Crusty blood and dirt clung to her thighs. The woman moaned again and Mikey tried turning his head but continued to stare in fascination at the woman's naked body.

"Help," she said. "Help me?"

Her words threw Mikey into action and he hopped back to the road and lit out for home at a dead out run.

Gert, Nathan and Mikey Wheat lived three miles from town on a small farm of only sixty acres…but it was free and clear. In 1931 anything free and clear of the banks was wealth and Gert felt secure that morning, almost wealthy as she stored the last of the season's produce in the mud-walled cellar under the kitchen. Jars of green beans, corn, peaches and peas stood like soldiers ready to defend her family over the winter. Gert smoothed an escaped strand of hair back and tucked it into the serviceable bun at the nape of her neck. Her family would survive the winter ahead no matter what it had in store.

She was humming as she lifted the lantern off the shelf, held it high to light the steps and climbed towards the kitchen. She was at the top before she heard Mikey gasping for breath and yelling, "Mama!"

Gert blew out the lantern, set it on the kitchen table and hurried toward the yelling. "Michael? What are you doing back here?'

"Mama," he gasped. "A woman...nearly dead...naked . . ." His face was pale in spite of the run.

"Slow down," his mother said. "Breathe!" She bent to circle his shoulders with a comforting arm. He shook it off.

"She's naked, Mama. Blood on her . . ." The whites of his eyes were large. "I think she's dying."

"Where?' his mother asked.

"The other side of the railroad tracks. In the tall grass."

Gert Wheat began gathering things together, a blanket, some bandages, a small jug of Nathan's whiskey. "Catch your breath a minute, Michael. Then run get your father. I think he's mending fence down by the creek. I'll go ahead to the track and look for her."

"You'll see the egg basket," Mikey said. A look of shame filled his eyes and his shoulders sagged. "I left the eggs."

"It's okay." She patted his arm. "Run get your father." And she started down the path toward the road at a brisk walk.

Mikey found his father only part way to the creek. "Probably a hobo," Nathan Wheat said. "Fell of a train or was pushed."

"A woman, daddy. It was a woman," Mikey said. "Naked."

Nathan took his son's hand. "We'll go see," he said. He left his tools and the two of them set off across the field, cutting at an angle for the tracks.

Gert found Eve just as Mikey and Nathan arrived. She looked like a baby bird thrown from the nest and left to die. With a glance at Mikey and a shake of her head at Nathan she signaled him to wait. She covered Eve with the blanket...wounds and all. Mikey edged forward trying to get another look.

Nathan put a hand on Mikey's shoulder. "How bad is it, Gert?" he asked.

"I'm not sure," she said. "Michael, you go on to town. Ask Doc Jones to stop by the house when he gets time and then go one to school."

"I found her, Mama. Can't I stay and see she's okay?"

"Do what your mother says." Nathan turned the boy toward the road.

"Don't forget the eggs," Gert said. The boy picked up the egg basket and headed down the road to town. When he looked back over his shoulder he could see his parents, heads bent close, talking seriously.

"We can't take her home," Nathan said. "A sick stranger in the house and winter coming on. I don't like it. Not one bit."

"You're right, Nathan. These are times to look after your own, but she's pregnant and she's hurt. We can't just leave her here." Gert's eyes were sad, confused. "Home is closer than town and it's just till she's recovered enough to move on."

Eve moaned, opened her eyes and tried to move. Gert crouched down and held Eve's good hand. "You're okay," she said. "But I'm going to splint your arm and it's going to hurt." Gert opened the jug of whiskey, Held Eve's head and gave her a drink.

Nathan found a sturdy stick, cut it to the proper length. The two of them straightened Eve's arm, bandaged it to the stick. The pain made Eve cry out and she fainted. They made a hammock from the blanket and with Gert at one end and Nathan at the other, they hoisted her up and carried her to their home. She was cleaned up, wearing one of Gert's soft night gowns and laying on crisp, cool sheets when she came to.

"Where am I?' Eve asked.

"You're in Edencrest, Ohio," Gert said, "Forty miles South of Columbus."

"I'm still in Ohio? I was trying to get to Florida or Georgia…some place warm," she said. "I was on the train… three men …," she said.

"Shhh," Gert said. "Don't think about it. Don't talk about it. Doc Jones will be here later to see how I did with setting your arm."

"It's broken?"

"Two places, I think, but it should heal fine." Gert clicked her tongue against the roof of her mouth. "I've got some broth for you --" Gert shook her head. "You're thin as a willow branch. You need to drink the broth and later I'll poach you a couple of eggs. You've got to eat something for the baby."

Eve's eyes met Gert's. "Is the baby okay?'

"Far as I can tell," Gert said. "Probably hungry though." She smiled, held the cup of broth and Eve sipped. The broth was rich, salty and certainly the most delicious thing Eve had tasted in her entire life.

Halloween passed, Eve woke only to sip some broth or eat a few bites. Gert stayed close to the house, Mikey spent evenings just watching her sleep and Nathan went about the business of the farm thin-lipped and disapproving. Doc

Jones stopped by once a week, stood over the bed and shook his head. "I don't know," he'd say. "She should be getting better by now.

Neighbors brought cakes and bread and stole glances at Eve through the bedroom door.

"Who is she?" they asked and Gert would shrug. "She hasn't told us anything yet."

By Thanksgiving Eve's arm had healed and bit by bit she told Gert the story of her life on the road. "Charlie will come for me," she said. "Charlie will come."

Gert shook her head and sighed. She doubted Charlie would ever come and if he did, could they feed another person?

When the cold, dark winter set in, neighbors stopped dropping by with food. Doc Jones didn't visit anymore and as January passed even Nathan's eyes became more accusing. Through it all Eve shared the Wheat's food and their fire. She ate but didn't regain her strength, she smiled but the joy was missing from her. Gert's love and care couldn't put back what the road had taken from her.

"I can't go on without Charlie," Eve said when she and Gert sat quietly, talking and sharing their lives.

"You have to do it," Gert said. "You have to do it for the baby."

Eve's hand lay on her protruding stomach. "Yes, the baby has to live," she said. Her eyes looked over Gert's head into some far unknown.

"A baby needs its mother. You have to live, too."

Eve shook her head. I've died a little every day since I went on the road. Charlie was all the strength I had. His child has to live...but me? I'm not important."

"Shhh," Gert said. "Don't even say those words."

"I know I've been a burden. You've been so kind, but I'm not strong like you." Tears formed in Eve's eyes.

Gert patted her hand, her tone softened. "You're strong enough," Gert said. "And motherhood will make you stronger."

"I don't think I'll make it," Eve said. "If I don't, promise me you'll look after the baby?"

"You'll make it. You have to."

"Promise me?"

"I can't promise you. There's Nathan to consider and Michael . . ."

"Don't promise if you can't but I trust you to do it. Be a good mother to my baby, teach him to be strong and true. Protect him from the bad things out there."

"You'll do those things yourself. I won't hear another word of this." Gert got up, left the warmth of the fire to check her own sleeping son. He was snoring softly in the safety of his room. Gert smoothed the covers over him.

On the Ides of March while the bitter winter of 1932 still had Ohio in its icy grip, Eve gave birth to Charlie Campbell, Jr. Gert cleaned the baby and held him up for Eve to see.

"He's beautiful," she said and held out her arms to take him.

Gert lay the baby on her chest. His lips smacked and he nuzzled into his mother looking for nourishment. Eve did her best but Gert took to supplementing the baby's diet with creamy fresh cow's milk. It meant there was little cream or butter for the family, but Charlie became pink and pudgy which made it seem a worthwhile sacrifice.

Mikey sat with the baby whenever he had a chance. "I've always wanted a brother," he said to Eve.

"Don't get too attached," Nathan said when he heard the words. "Eve and Charlie will be moving on one of these days." But even he was smiling when he passed the cradle and looking over Gert's shoulder when she fed the baby. Eve still lay abed most of the day and her strength hadn't returned. A fever blazed in her cheeks. Nathan and Mikey went to town to fetch Doc Jones.

"You love him, don't you?" Eve said as Gert wiped her face with a damp cloth.

"You know I do."

"And Nathan and Mikey?"

"They love him, too."

"You'll take care of him?"

Gert didn't answer but tears formed in her eyes.

"You are my only friend and Charlie's, too." Eve said. "Promise me?"

"I promise, Eve," Gert said. Eve held up her arms and Gert took the baby. Before Doc arrived, Eve had died.

"I promised Eve we'd raise the baby like he was our own." Gert said.

Nathan looked at Gert, he saw the smile on Mikey's face. "It's the least we can do," he said.

FROM THIS MOMENT ON
San Francisco, California October 14, 1943

Dear Grandma Rose,

Thank you for understanding about my marriage to James. I knew I could count on you the minute you said, *"Each life is made up of special moments, Ellen. Don't miss yours."* I hope Mum and Daddy are recovered from their shock and anger. I promise I'll make it right when I get home.

It feels like a whirlwind has caught up the whole country and set people flying in all directions. There are travelers everywhere. I only got put off the train once on the way to San Francisco. Some others weren't so lucky. I was put off in St. Louis along with twenty other wives going to see our husbands off. We spent the night and got on another train at 8 am the next morning. There were no empty hotels or rooms so I spent the night on a marble bench in the lady's room and was perfectly safe, though not very warm and not very comfortable. Everybody is having to make do and nobody is complaining. The trains are full of soldiers and sailors and they are looking after us.

I rode to St. Louis sitting next to a sailor from Georgia who'd never been away from his home county till he went to the Great Lakes Naval Training Station. His wife hasn't been able to visit because she is expecting a baby any day. He asked me to write a letter for him to send to her. Can you believe, Grandma, the poor man could neither read nor write? And then he asked to hold my hand and I said yes to both his small requests.

It's sad and exciting and frightening at the same time. Like a dream you don't want to wake up from because the war is out there and the Germans and the Japs and all our poor, dear boys leaving home to protect us.

You wouldn't believe San Francisco. Very warm even now and there are crowds on the streets at all hours. I never saw so many people in my life. James and I found a room for $10.00 a week...very steep- but we were lucky to get it. We are treasuring every moment. Who knows when we will see one another again.

We were able to get a line through to James' parents on Thursday. I think they wish we'd waited till the war was over to get married, too, but they were polite and welcomed me to the family over the phone. I hope I will be able to get to Indiana to meet them or better yet, I hope James gets home very soon and he can take me there to meet them.

I met James' buddy Treece. He's from Cleveland and also very handsome in his uniform. He isn't married yet, but has a girl at home. He had no problem finding girls to talk and dance with when we've gone out. I'm so happy to be here for James. To be the one he's spending his last days and nights in America with. Oh, Grandma Rose, I love him so much. I think my heart will break when he ships out. We have four more days.

Your loving granddaughter,
Ellen Goodman Morehouse
Mrs. James Morehouse (I get shivers just writing this)

Columbus, Ohio
December 23, 1943

My Darling Husband,

I love you and I miss you. My friend Barbara Brooks and I have found jobs in Columbus and are sharing a room during the week in Mrs. Peterson's home on the west side of town. She has four other girls living with her during the week. Just Barbara and I are from Edencrest. We will be going home tomorrow for Christmas. Usually Barbara and I ride the bus home on Friday evenings but because of the holiday are taking an extra day off this week. We had to work on Thanksgiving. That's how serious we are taking the war effort here in Ohio.

Sometimes we don't get home till after 10:00 PM because the in-town bus has to make it's runs and then the same bus makes an out of town run and that is the one we have to take. Nobody complains because we know it is helping out with the war effort. And it's much better than having daddy use his gasoline stamps to come pick us up, though he would be willing to do that for us.

Seven letters from your dear hands were delivered last week. They were dated October 18 through November 12, 1943 so the mail delay is six to eight weeks. I pray my letters are getting through to you. I write three times a week without fail. We listen to Walter Winchell every night hoping to get news of the Seventh Fleet, but all the news is of Europe. Most of it is not good.

I had a note from your mother last week. I'm going to try to go to Indianapolis in the spring. She asked me to come for a visit when I could get away. She sounds like a dear woman, James and I love her even though we haven't met yet. I know she has to be wonderful to have raised a man like you.

I wish I knew where you are, James. The Philippines, New Guinea, Australia. Such faraway places, such strange sounding names. We hear about General MacArthur and Admiral Nimitz and "Hap" Arnold but we all know you and the others like you are winning this war. We are depending on you to keep us safe.

Mum and daddy had a letter from my brother, Bill. He's in France and says things are tough there right now. The censors had marked through so many words and phrases, it was hard to make sense of the letter but we know he is alive and well, though he says sometimes the food is scarce and the fighting is fierce. I wish you had met Bill, but there will be time for all that later.

Lawrence Carmichael has filed as a Conscientious Objector and people in Edencrest cross the street when he walks by. They've put a sign in the barbershop window that says, *"Lawrence Carmichael, other yellow-bellies and skunks not welcome here"*. Lawrence has always been a gentle soul...wouldn't dissect a frog in biology class when we were in school and I'm sure never hurt a living thing. It's sad to see him so alone in his own home town. With everybody else working so hard to win this war, he's chosen a very hard row to hoe. He says he'd rather die himself than take the life of another human being. He may have to leave town or go to jail before this is over.

I hope this letter and all the love I send with it reaches you by Christmas. We are going to go to church and have a quiet dinner at home to celebrate and, of course, I will be thinking of you, my sweet love.

Your Adoring Wife,

Ellen

Edencrest, Ohio
April 18, 1944

My dear James,

Your mother and father were most gracious to me on my recent visit. They let me sleep in your old room which was a treat for me. I hope you don't mind my looking through the books on your shelf. I didn't know you were such a Jack London fan. It made me stop and think how many things I don't know about you yet.

It seems I've known you all my life and it's been just over nine months and six of those you've been gone. Your mother has left your clothes in the dresser drawers and I pulled them out, James, and buried my face in the shirts that belong to you. I want to know everything about you...every detail of your life before we met.

Your mother showed me the photographs in the family album. You were a beautiful, pudgy baby. I want to have several that look just like you one of these days. And I loved the photo of you at five with the fish you caught at Lake Tippecanoe. The fish was as big as you, James. Your mother laughed telling how it almost pulled you off the dock before your father helped you land it.

I liked your parents. They are such warm, loving people and I'm so happy to have learned about your growing up. I want to hear all the same stories from you when you get home.

Spring is such a hopeful time of year to me. Grandma Rose came to help Mum put in the garden. I asked them to leave some of the planting till Saturday, so I could help. Mum had the garden plowed ten feet wider this year and we'll be putting in more corn and green beans. Even in Ohio where we've always had gardens, now we have Victory Gardens. As I planted the seeds, I prayed you'd be here to help with the harvest or at the latest by Christmas, so you can help eat the things I'm planting. The soil is such a big part of my stability and I never feel closer to God than when I'm working in the soil.

My cousin, Becky Goodman has a new baby boy. Her husband is in Europe, like Bill. She named the baby Isaiah Brentwood Goodman after his grandfather and Grandma Rose (Brentwood was her maiden name). Such a big name for such a little fellow, James. I took a set of booties Mum knit and visited on Sunday. I wish we had a baby on the way, James. Babies make me feel very hopeful, too. We'll have time for all that when this war is over.

Loved the photo you sent of you and Treece and the two children standing under the palm tree. It must have been in New Guinea but the description you wrote on the back of the picture was inked out and we couldn't be sure.

All my love and kisses,

Ellen

Columbus, Ohio
August 2, 1944

Dear James,

I haven't been home to Edencrest since June. We are working seven days a week at the plant. I got a promotion and a ten cents an hour raise. I'm not making as much as a man in the same job but I'll be able to save a little more each week toward our house. I dream of the day we'll be together under our own roof.

Your mother got a line through to Mrs. Peterson's yesterday. She asked if I'd heard from you. Neither of us has had a letter in over three months. I'm not complaining, but the days drag by when we are waiting for mail. We all miss you, James and love you more than words can say. We know you have been at sea for a long time. I hope our letters are reaching you.

There are only four of us left at Mrs. Peterson's and we sit together in the evenings as we are too tired to go out. Mrs. Peterson is teaching me how to knit and I'm hoping to send you a surprise made with my own hands for Christmas. I have my own room now and when I'm alone at night, I think of you and our sweet time together.

Mum sent a note that daddy has been heading up a scrap drive at home. People are gathering up every scrap of metal and they even pulled Austin Bright's truck out of the Scioto River, hosed it down and turned it in. You wouldn't know about Austin's truck but everyone in Edencrest does.

Austin had too much to drink one Saturday night and ran his old, Ford truck off the Main Street Bridge. Austin nearly drowned, had to kick out the front windshield with his boot to escape and swore he'd never drive again. He threatened to shoot anyone who tried to haul the truck out of the river and since it was held together by baling twine and fence wire, nobody even tried till now. Mum said half the town came to watch and it was so mired down it took a four-horse team to pull it out. Austin was there and gave a little speech saying he'd decided not to shoot anyone. He just hoped the truck got made into guns and would do some shooting for him.

We're all behind you, James. I hope you know this.

Gert Wheat joined the Gold Star Mothers last week. Her son, Michael died somewhere in the Pacific. He was only eighteen and always such a serious, responsible boy. That is fourteen Gold Star Mothers now from our little town. Everyone dreads the sight of a telegram messenger these days.

Stay safe for me, James and know that I pray every day for your return.

Your loving wife,

Ellen

Columbus, Ohio
November 29, 1944

My Dear James,

I'm twenty-two now. Mrs. Peterson was able to get together enough flour, sugar and chocolate to make a small cake. I suspect she got the ingredients from

Mr. Black which I don't approve of. She was so pleased with the cake, I hadn't the heart to question her about it. Mum sent some eggs back with me when I was home for Thanksgiving, so we had a small omelet and the cake. All of it a celebration.

I feel quite mature and competent after what we've been through, and very aware of the passage of time. I've been thinking a lot of Grandma Rose's words about living the moments of our life as they come to us. I'm grateful not to have missed our moments together as husband and wife. I hope I'm not an old, wrinkled woman before we are together again.

Your recent letters were a boost to me. They contained the stories of your liberty in Australia. I'm grateful you had no more damage than a black eye. I think you should save your fighting for the Japs.

Mum hasn't heard from Bill in over seven weeks and mail is usually faster than that from Europe. I can see she is frightened for his safety. Last we heard he was in Italy.

The worst for me is not knowing where you are. We've heard news of the Seventh Fleet in a huge battle in the Philippines. It is being called the Battle of Leyte Gulf. Casualties were heavy according to the first reports and I am praying you survived, if you were there.

The news is sounding better to us here at home. It's hard to tell how much is true and how much might be propaganda to prop us up. Shortages are everywhere. Daddy has gone to printing the Blade only every third day because of the paper shortage. We depend on the radio for news of the war and important local news travels by word of mouth faster than the paper can be printed.

Oh, James, I'm afraid for all of us. We are changing in ways we can't even recognize, yet. I fear life will never go back to normal...that this will never be over and most of all that I will never see you again.

Stay safe for me, my darling,

Ellen

Columbus, Ohio
January 5, 1943

My Darling James,

Your letters arrived yesterday. I took them to my room, sat on my bed and wept before I got up the courage to open them. Barbara and I saw film of the

Philippines battles at the movies before Christmas. The film was frightening… terrifying…but when I read your words, James, I cried even harder. The battle had to be horrible and with no sleep for seventy hours. I don't know how you stood it. But the saddest, most joyous thing was your carrying the poor, dear boys too weak to walk out of the prisons. When I think of their families, the people who love them, maybe thinking they were dead, hearing the news that they are alive. You and all the sailors in the entire U.S. Navy are heroes.

I cannot imagine the noise of the battle that you describe and we know of the sinking of the Princeton. You were only two ships away? My knees go weak at the thought. Surely total victory can't be far in the future.

I hate to tell you but Bill is MIA and daddy is inconsolable. Mum is more worried about daddy, than Bill. I can tell, though she shrugs and goes to church each morning to pray for Bill's safety. I wish I could be home to help them both but my work here is too important to walk away from. My heart is divided by the concern I feel for all of you.

Mum says there are already nineteen Gold Star mothers in Edencrest and she refuses to be number twenty. That's her position on Bill. I pray she is right.

All we have to do now is hold ourselves together till it's over. We're going to win; the world is going to be safe again. We just have to hold on till it happens. Our dreams are still possible, James. They will come true.

All My Love,

Ellen

Columbus, Ohio
April 14, 1945

James Dear,

The nation is mourning. Eleanor has been braver than many of the rest of us. President Truman doesn't roll off my tongue like President Roosevelt did. He's the only president I can remember. There is so much change to absorb.

I feel at sea, myself and long for something firm and solid under my feet. I long to go home...to wake up and look out the window of my room and see the apple orchard, the barn and the beauty of growing things in the distance. I'm tired of war, James. My prayers are for peace, your safe return and definite word about Bill.

Lawrence Carmichael is back home in Edencrest. He spent eighteen months working in a mental hospital in Michigan. It seems unfair he is home before those of you who agreed to fight for our country. Mum says nobody pays much attention to him. The sign in the barbershop window is long gone and people seem almost glad to see him, like he's been off to a war of his own.

So much has changed so quickly. We've lived the moments of our lives half a world apart James, but there have been some wonderful, rich moments for me. I can cry with joy feeling the end is near. I know I'll be seeing you soon.

Your Loving Wife,

Ellen

Columbus, Ohio
May 14, 1945

Good News James,

Bill was in a prison camp. He is safe, if not well and will be sent home as soon as he's strong enough to travel.

Daddy put the news in a half inch headline on the front page of the Blade. Mum says he's like he was when he was twenty-five. A spring in his step and a smile for everyone. A cloud has been lifted from the world and from my father. Mussolini is dead, Hitler is dead and my brother is alive.

The only other thing I need is you here in my arms, James. I pray it will happen soon.

Love,

Ellen

Edencrest, Ohio
June 20, 1945

Darling James,

The Army has invaded Edencrest. Barbara and I came home for three days just to see it. Work has slowed at the plant and they could spare us. More of the boys who were in Europe are coming home nearly every day. Most have thirty days leave before they have to return to duty and some, like Bill, are home on extended leave. It was pure luck he arrived while we were here. I had to wait my turn to hug him, James, but it was worth it.

Daddy cried like a baby…like a baby, James. I've never seen him shed a tear in his life and he wept like a child. We all did.

Bill is pitifully thin, but well. Mum started cooking almost the moment he walked through the door and hasn't stopped yet. There has been a parade of people through the house to welcome him home. He smiles and greets everyone politely but something about him still seems far away.

I came upon him sitting in the swing out back this morning. He was wearing old overalls that hung in folds on his skinny frame and tears rolled down his cheeks as he looked out at the fields. I felt embarrassed to intrude on him, but he motioned me to sit in the swing with him, so I did. We didn't talk but he held my hand and we swung back and forth for nearly an hour, just being home together. I noticed him wiping tears now and then but I let that be for him. It was a wonderful but very strange thing to sit there beside him and feel so separated from him at the same time.

I'm thinking of going back to Columbus just to get my things from Mrs. Peterson's. I believe my job there is finished. Men are home to take our places. I know Japan is yet to be defeated but the starch has gone out of me. I want to get back to my real life here in Edencrest, or what is left of it. I pray daily for your speedy return.

All My Love,

Ellen

Edencrest, Ohio
August 15, 1945

My Beloved James,

Word of Japan's surrender reached us today. Pandemonium broke out on Main Street and the celebration got bigger as more people heard. There was an impromptu parade…people who had gasoline drove through town honking horns and alerting those who hadn't heard.

Daddy called us from the Blade office and Mum and I picked up Grandma Rose and drove to town to join in the celebration.

Lawrence Carmichael was driving the fire truck up Main Street, turning around and driving back the other way. He was clanging the bell most of the time and I saw John Goodman give him a mug of beer that he drank hanging out the window of the fire truck.

People were dancing in the street and I was kissed and hugged more times than I could count. Even Grandma Rose danced and I don't mind telling you she cut a fine figure.

Bill and I went to the Presbyterian Church and said a prayer of Thanksgiving that it's over...finally over. We weren't the only ones there but eventually everyone was back on the streets.

Daddy bought drinks for every man in town, I think. Austin Bright, after having several, jumped off the Main Street Bridge and broke both his legs. He vowed never to swim again.

James, we have a life to live. I'm counting the moments till you are home.

Forever Yours,

Ellen

LOVE THY NEIGHBOR
Third Base Dugout 1952
Edencrest Eagles Ball Diamond

Ruth Ann Brooks was a lot like the town of Edencrest. She looked proper and in control on the surface but underneath there were things that smoldered and threatened to explode. Two things kept Ruth Ann from loosening herself. First, her daddy, a good man, was the preacher at the Edencrest First Methodist Church. Second was Hell. Ruth Ann hadn't completely done away with the possibility of Hell.

She'd decided last year, when she was just fifteen, that the idea of virginity was over-rated but she'd be darned if she was going to lose hers to the likes of Bobby Weaver who didn't even have a car. His mother was a war widow who had to work part-time at the cash register of Jordan's Market to make ends meet. And she wasn't going to lose it tonight in this awful August heat. But Bobby was coming on strong and it would be so easy . . .

Ruth Ann could feel the heat of the day still trapped in the dugout's cement blocks as she leaned back against them. Bobby's lips worked on hers and the callused hardness of his thick fingers was urgent under her blouse. She could feel the sensations clear to her toes.

Times like this Ruth Ann forgot her daddy, the Edencrest First Methodist Church and just about everything else she'd ever known. But she had to remember the time (so there'd be no questions when she got home) and she had to remember to keep Bobby's hands above her waist. The one time she'd let him touch her down there, she'd completely lost control. Thank goodness Bobby did too. He'd come all over her leg but she'd worried two long weeks wondering if she was pregnant. She wasn't 100% clear on reproductive details, but she was sure she didn't want any part of being pregnant with Bobby Weaver. That would mean marriage, an eternal yoke around her neck and Bobby's rough hands on her any time he wanted.

Ruth Ann's sights were set on some of Edencrest's bigger fish—Richard Goodman or Skippy Jordan—boys with class and brighter prospects.

Bobby moved his hand to Ruth Ann's knee and is was headed north when she heard the hollow thump of bare feet on hard-packed dirt. Ruth Ann stiffened. Bobby Weaver didn't notice.

"Bobby," she said. "Someone's out there."

He mumbled something she couldn't understand and nuzzled her ear.

Ruth Ann clamped her knees together and pushed his head away from hers. "Listen."

"Aw, Ruthie, it's nothing," Bobby said. He adjusted his position on the dugout bench and went after her lips again.

This time she used both hands to push him away. "Look over there."

Bobby peered into the darkness. "Just the Carmichael kid," he said. "Probably cutting through to the filling station to get a bottle of pop."

Ruth Ann could see the small figure hot-footing it past second base, then she heard the clatter of others vaulting the third base fence. More feet beat down the hard-packed baseline.

"Get the little commie fucker," a voice yelled and before the smaller boy could reach the outfield, they did.

Masculine huffs of heavy breathing and the small boy's whimpers carried on the warm night air. Ruth Ann sat up straight, adjusted her blouse and skirt. "Do you think they can see us?" she asked.

"Naw," Bobby drawled. "They're too busy to notice us." He tried slipping a hand back under Ruth Ann's skirt.

"No," she said. Her eyes were on the scene unfolding in the Edencrest outfield.

"C'mon Ruthie. You've got to be home in a half hour and you got me all stirred up."

"You got yourself stirred up, Bobby Weaver and you know it. I didn't do a thing. Now be quiet. They'll hear you."

"Gonna teach you red, commie bastards a lesson," a voice said.

"Can you tell who it is?" Ruth Ann asked.

"Looks like the Carmichael kid to me." Bobby said.

"Not him. The other one."

"Could be trouble to know," he said.

"You a coward?" Ruth Ann said. "Watch while three big guys beat up a kid? Tommy Carmichael's in third grade."

"Kid's gotta learn, too," Bobby said. "Besides his dad is a commie who wouldn't fight in a war that got my old man killed." Bobby slid his arm around Ruth Ann's shoulder, tried to pull her in for a kiss, but the mood was broken.

She crossed her arms over her chest. "Soon as they leave, I want to go home. It's dangerous meeting you here. My father thinks I'm at Sarah Johnson's house working on an MYF project."

Bobby slumped back against the dugout wall and Ruth Ann leaned forward to watch the commotion in the outfield.

"Gonna teach your daddy a lesson, boy." The voice crackled with anger. "Hold him down," it said. The small figure kicked and rolled while the bigger one's tried to pin him to the ground.

"Ow! The little fucker bit my hand," one said and there was a loud grunt as one dark figure kicked the boy on the ground.

"I have to do it all," the angry voice said, then he pulled a flask from his back pocket and poured liquid from it over the still figure.

"Awful waste of your daddy's whiskey, Rich," one said.

"There's plenty," the angry voice said. He put the flask to his lips, took a drink, then passed it and stood back. Ruth Ann could see the bright flame of a match and then the soft glow of a cigarette against the darkness of the night. The smell of alcohol wafted over the dugout.

"They're going to set him on fire," Ruth Ann said. Her breath caught in her throat and she fought the urge to scream.

Bobby clamped a hand over her mouth. "Shut the fuck up," he said.

The boy with the cigarette stepped back and flipped the match at the small figure on the ground. Two ran and the thump of their feet hung in the air. The flame from the match spread and engulfed Tommy Carmichael in a blue flame.

Ruth Ann jerked away from Bobby, screamed and ran toward the burning boy. Bobby swore, hopped the third base fence and headed for home.

Rich Goodman stood by while Ruth Ann spread her skirt over Tommy, fell to her knees and rolled him into it to smother the flames. He took a final pull from the flask he still held in his hand and flicked the butt into the grass.

"Now why'd you go and do that?" he asked Ruth Ann. "His father is a Red. He deserves to die."

"He's a little boy," Ruth Ann said. "He needs a doctor."

Rich shrugged.

"You're not afraid of getting caught, are you?"

"No," Rich said. "My father is the Mayor. He owns everything worth having in this town. Nobody's going to touch me."

Ruth Ann unrolled the little boy, stepped back into her burned skirt. "He could die, you know."

"That was the plan until you came along, sweet pea," Rich said.

"Then you'd be a murderer."

Rich laughed. "No," he said. "I'd still be the Mayors son."

Ruth Ann lifted the limp boy into her arms. "I might tell."

Rich reached out and touched her cheek with the back of his hand. "I'm not worried, sweet pea." He grinned. "I saw Bobby Weaver hightail it out of here and I've got something to tell, too."

Ruth Ann turned her back and trudged toward the lights of the filling station, Tommy Carmichael whimpering in her arms.

Ninety minutes later Ruth Ann was sitting on a hard, wooden bench in the Edencrest Police Station watching the aftermath of tragedy unfold. Her skirt was torn and black, there were scorch marks on her blouse, but her feet were planted primly on the floor. Her father was on his way.

Tommy Carmichael was already in the burn unit of Children's Hospital forty miles away. A disheveled Chief Witherspoon paced back and forth, a phone plastered to his over-sized ear. Patrolman Eddie Harris stood nearby sneaking peeks at Ruth Ann's tattered garments.

Witherspoon finally said, "Yeah, good. Thanks Doc." And clunked the phone into its cradle. He turned to Harris. "The kid's going to live. Some of the burns on his face are third degree." The Chief shook his head. "I saw burns in the war and his face will probably end up puckered and red as the mayor's asshole."

Eddie blushed and nodded toward Ruth Ann. "Oh," Witherspoon said. "Forgot she was here." He glanced at Ruth Ann. "Sorry for the language."

Ruth Ann smiled.

"What's keeping the preacher?" Witherspoon asked. "I been here a half hour already."

"I called you first," Harris said. "Figured we had a murder on our hands."

The Chief nodded. "You coulda been right. And the kid coulda set hisself on fire and miss preacher's kid coulda been passing by the ball field, but I don't believe any of it." He shook his head. "Damn kids get wilder every year. No respect!"

Ruth Ann shifted uncomfortably on the bench and stared at her scraped knees. She pursed her lips together and silently vowed never to confess to necking in the dugout with Bobby Weaver, even if Tommy Carmichael died and the cops charged her with his murder.

Her father arrived, his worried face nearly hanging in folds. Ruth Ann had never seen him look so old. "You okay, honey?" he asked reaching for her hand.

Ruth Ann shrugged and nodded to her father.

"What's going on?" His eyes looked heavenward and his voice had the same tremulous, nearly teary quality it took on in Sunday morning prayer.

"She saved Tommy Carmichael's life," Witherspoon said. "Though I doubt he's going to thank her for it when he gets a good look at hisself."

"Lawrence's boy?" the Reverend said in a tone that seemed to make it all seem reasonable.

"Yeah! Somebody set him on fire. She smothered the flames with her skirt and carried him all the way from the ball field to the filling station to get help."

"The ball field? What was she doing at the ball field?" Reverend Brooks turned and looked at his daughter. "What were you doing at the ball field, Ruth Ann?"

"Just walking, daddy. Taking the long way home and thinking about the MYF project Sarah and I were working on."

This time the Chief looked towards heaven and shrugged.

"So what's the problem, here Frank? Are you holding my daughter or can I take her home?"

"Not holding her exactly, Reverend, but the Doc's in Columbus say the boy was on fire only about three minutes and unless he set hisself, there'd have had to be others around and , ummm, they think he was doused in alcohol first."

"Alcohol?"

"Yeah, you know…whiskey, vodka, gin…or it could have been rubbing alcohol. But sounds like there may have been a party going on, the kid wandered in and things got out of hand." The chief shrugged. "We keep an eye out for that sort of thing," he shrugged again, "But kids have been known to play around, drink and neck down at the ball field…let off steam, you know."

The Reverend's eyes popped open and his eyebrows peaked. "Ruth Ann has no steam to let off. She's a young girl, hardly raised to drink and neck in a public place…or a private one for that matter."

Witherspoon shrugged again. "Hot summer night. I could use a cold one myself." Harris coughed and the Reverend took Ruth Ann's arm, pulled her up from the bench. "We're going home…sounds like she's a hero to me."

Sunday dawned hot and humid. Ruth Ann's clothes stuck to her as soon as she put them on. She wadded up her burned skirt and tossed it in the trash. She hurried because she had to talk to Sarah Johnson before her father or Chief Witherspoon.

She waited outside the church smiling at the Methodists as they filed in and when Sarah arrived in the back seat of her parents green Oldsmobile, Ruth Ann hurried towards the car, grabbed Sarah and pulled her to one side.

"Don't be late for the processional," Mrs. Johnson said. The girls smiled and nodded.

"You've got to promise to say I was at your house last night till 9:15," Ruth Ann said.

"You didn't set Tommy Carmichael on fire did you?" Sarah's eyes were big as she asked.

You heard already?"

"It was in the Blade this morning. My Dad said it was good enough for him."

"You promise?"

"You know I do." Sarah said. "I always promise and nobody ever asks."

"They might this time." Ruth Ann said. I was there and saw the whole thing with Tommy. And they held me at the police station till my dad came."

Sarah's eyes were wide. "Your dad had to pick you up at the police station?"

"Yeah," Ruth Ann said. "My skirt half burned to shreds and Eddie Harris eyeing me the entire time."

"You didn't do it, did you?"

"No, I didn't do it, but I know who did."

"No problem on my end," Sarah said. "My parents were at the Country Club till after midnight and I heard daddy staggering up the stairs AGAIN."

"Good," Ruth Ann said. "You're a true friend."

"What if Bobby talks?"

"He won't. He was too chicken to stay and help. He won't want anybody to know he ran. Trust me, I know Bobby Weaver. Besides, he doesn't know who did it."

The girls slipped into the last pew of the church just as the organ swelled into the opening bars of the processional hymn.

The Reverend Brooks scripture for the day was Leviticus 19:18 and he told the congregation he'd stayed up all night preparing the message after learning of the burning of Tommy Carmichael.

The Methodists fanning themselves with cardboard cut-outs of Christ, sat tall in their pews and listened politely.

"Thou shalt not avenge the children of thy people," he said. "But thou shalt love they neighbor as thyself."

Ruth Ann searched out the back of Richard Goodman's head as her father spoke of the prosperity of freedom, respect for differences and forgiveness of what is past. Her father's words were impassioned and his message was clear to the Edencrest faithful who shifted uneasily on the hard, wooden pews. Sweat trickled down spines, eyes wandered and attention flitted away.

The congregation's mood hung in the heavy air of the sanctuary. Hadn't Lawrence Carmichael refused to fight for the freedom he now expected to enjoy? Didn't he go to Columbus each and every month for a meeting he refused to talk about? Wasn't it odd he buried his trash when everybody else in town hauled it to the city dump for all to see? It didn't take Senator Joe McCarthy to search out every communist sympathizer in the country. An eye for an eye would have been a more appropriate scripture for this morning.

They all knew Ruth Ann had sat in Chief Witherspoon's jail for two hours last night before she was allowed to go home. Tommy Carmichael had refused to identify his attackers and Bobby Weaver had some things to say about Ruth Ann Brooks as well.

Spines stiffened, papers rustled and hymnals thumped prematurely into their slots. Richard Goodman swiveled his head around and grinned broadly at Ruth Ann. By the time it was over she knew there would be calls from the bishop, tears from her mother and naive disbelief from her father.

The town had closed ranks against them and they were now on the outside with the Carmichaels. Her father had paved the way out in solid gold. Even Sarah sat straighter and leaned away form her. Ruth Ann knew all promises were off. She wanted to stand and scream but instead she joined a few wavering voices in the recessional and even smiled when Sarah said she had to hurry or she'd miss her ride home.

Ruth Ann filed out of church with the rest of the worshipers and like them she avoided her father standing at the door of the sanctuary—an embarrassed smile plastered on his face.

Richard Goodman grabbed her by the elbow and said, "You should have let him burn, sweet pea."

Ruth Ann nodded and knew that Hell was real.

MOVING ON FROM EDENCREST

THE MISSING BARITONE

I am an old woman now, dying slowly...day by day. The doctors say the cancer is speeding up the process. My days are hazy, clouded by drugs and pain, but there are memories, clear and clean as a spring morning after rain...not all of them are good.

My mother was formidable, a big woman, with shoulders broad enough to swing an ax, one of eleven children born to a half-breed Indian woman and a tall wiry man with sunken cheeks and mean, piercing eyes. My mother had a picture of them taken in the front yard of the house where she grew up. It was a two-room shack, with a yard of dirt... just plain dirt...Not a blade of grass or a single flower. In the picture there are children scattered around. One is sitting on a mule.

When I misbehaved as a child, she showed me the picture.

"A woman's life is hard," she said. "I want better for you."

It was her excuse for everything.

My father was a railroad man who worked when times were hard. He was even taller and broader than my mother… and gruff. It was the way of fathers to be gruff and not always trying to please their children like they do today. Thanks to his job and my mother's hard work we were never hungry and we were never cold. Many were. We lived in a big house, south of Main Street. Nothing grand, but I had a room all my own with windows to the south and east. There was a yard with grass and flowers, cherry trees and apples and some currant bushes...(I loved currants)...lilacs and a willow tree. We had chickens and a cow and out beside the chicken house was a truck patch where my mother and I coaxed green beans, potatoes, corn and carrots to flourish under the summer sun. But still, from an early age, I braced myself against the world.

I was my mother's first born, but she liked my brother best. His name was Roy which means King and she always called him, "My sweet little Roy". Roy experienced the world through his mouth. He would eat and he would sing.

"We'll bake a currant pie for my sweet Roy."

I helped my mother pick the currants, stemmed and washed them and baked them into pies. "Cut the lard into the flour, Rachel," my mother said. "Let the water run cold before you add it to the dough. Cold water makes a crust flaky...and roll it thin...the thinner, the better."

She taught me many things.

The smell of currants and cinnamon filled our big old kitchen like honeysuckle filled the warm night air. As the pies baked my mouth ran wet with anticipation.

"We have to let them cool a bit," she said when she pulled them from the oven. She ruffled Roy's hair where he sat on a tall stool watching; singing softly; smiling. My mother sent me running to Moore's Grocery two blocks off to get ice cream. I swear I ran so fast the buckles on my shoes got warm.

When I got back Roy was still sitting; singing; watching the pies. My mother was busy with other things. He ran his fat pink tongue over the tops of the pies leaving a track in the sparkling sugar, his greedy eyes on mine all the while.

"Mother," I yelled. "Roy licked the pies again."

And she came, skirt tail snapping as she walked, "My sweet little Roy loves currant pie." She pulled him into her bosom and hugged him hard. "Now let's all have some."

I ate the ice cream carefully from around the pie, and lifted the crust I'd labored over to seek out the currants underneath thinking of my brother's grotesque pink tongue.

I never had a second piece.

I was twelve when my mother told me about a man...a man I presumed afterward to be my father. She showed me a picture of him, too. Brown with age by then and curled around the edges. A hard-looking man, wearing a hat with the brim turned down putting his face in shadow. It made me wild to think of my mother coming on the train from Illinois to marry the man I knew as my father with me already germinating inside of her. Looking back I suppose it made me angry, too, to be so different from my brother, somehow less entitled to the benefits provided by a man with no blood connection. I wondered if he knew this secret from my mother's heart. I wondered whether I was born of love...or rape and anger... fear perhaps.

Roy was a big boy, tall like my mother but soft and girlish around the edges. My mother dressed him in knickers that buckled at the knee. It was ordinary in those days and ordinary that when a boy reached the age of twelve or so, he'd graduate to long pants. When the time came we all bundled into Mrs. Pettijohn's coupe to make the trip to Indianapolis. Mrs. Pettijohn was our neighbor from across the street. She and my mother sat in the front seat gossiping about mutual acquaintances while Roy, Beth Pettijohn and I crowded into the back, giggling behind our hands, quietly poking one another as we rode.

The tailor showed my mother several pairs of long pants. She made a selection and sent Roy into the dressing room to try them on.

"Hurry up, Roy," my mother said through the curtain when he took too long coming back.

"I don't like them," he said.

"Put them on," my mother said with a pleading tone. "Mrs. Pettijohn has other things to do." She flashed an embarrassed smile at the tailor and at Mrs. Pettijohn. My mother, for all her power, did not like to be out of control in any situation.

"I don't like them," came again from behind the privacy curtain. This time a whine.

Mrs. Pettijohn took Beth by the hand and led her to a display of fancy ties and shirt buttons. She fingered them gingerly, her back to the family crisis. The tailor shifted from foot to foot and stared at the floor. I bit my tongue to keep from giggling.

"You get out here," my mother said, "or I'm coming in."

Silence from my brother.

My mother glanced furtively at the tailor, squared her shoulders and whipped back the privacy curtain. My brother was standing there still in his knickers, the long pants a wrinkled ball in the corner.

She went for Roy's belt, which he protected furiously. "I don't like them," he yelled. She wrestled him to the floor and still he protected himself with knees bent into his chest…soft, round buttocks rolling on the floor. My mother held Roy there and looked over her shoulder. A hank of hair had fallen loose and wisped across her nose.

I stood watching.

"Close the curtain, girl," she said and I did…leaving myself alone to return the tailor's stare.

Behind the curtain there was heavy breathing. Thumping sounds. Silence. When they emerged my mother's face was pale and Roy was still wearing his knickers. She held him tightly by the hand and addressed the tailor. "We'll come again another day."

The tailor nodded without a word and my mother jerked Roy's arm and lead him out of the store. On the ride home he sat between my mother and Mrs. Pettijohn in the front seat of the car singing and Beth and I giggled in the back.

When I was old enough and the juices began to flow in me, I'd climb out my bedroom window and run wild through the night with other kids from town. Roy had been coaxed into long pants by this time and started singing lessons with Mrs. Jones from the high school. My mother gave him the job of watching to keep me out of trouble.

My hair was dark and coarse as a Shawnee warrior, but I bobbed it in the style of the day. It curled into my chin and swung smartly when I moved my head. I felt like a woman though I was only sixteen. Anger had grown in me and I liked it that boys paid attention to me.

The warm summer air was velvet on my skin as I climbed out my bedroom window and ran through shadows to meet Beth Pettijohn under the big sycamore tree. I looked over my shoulder as we headed toward Main Street but there was no sign of Roy and there was no sound of his singing. It was a special treat to sneak away from him. Beth and I giggled and held hands as we walked. My hair bounced against my cheeks.

That night there was a carload of boys, four of them, from over near Dunkirk roaring around the streets. They were in Malcolm Carter's convertible and looked sweet as a bucket full of syrup. Malcolm slowed the car so it rolled along at the same speed Beth and I were walking. Malcolm was close enough to us that I could have reached out and touched him.

"Nice night," he said.

Beth and I looked at one another and bit our lips to keep from giggling.

"Nice enough," I said sticking out my chest.

"Been walking far?" Malcolm asked.

"Far enough," I said. Beth squeezed my hand and giggled.

"We'd be pleased to give you a ride over to the park," Malcolm said.

"Why would we want to go to the park?" I said.

"Take a walk; sit under the pergola and talk, anything you want," Malcolm said. The rest of the boys banged on the side of the car and laughed.

I stopped and looked straight into Malcolm's eyes. They were blue and his eyelids crinkled at the corners. Deep dimples creased his cheeks. "Well, it seems we're already walking and we're already talking, " I said and smiled my best vamp smile.

"We got some beer," Malcolm said and held up two brown bottles.

"There's only two of us," Beth said.

"No problem," Malcolm said and two of the boys hopped out of the car and held the doors for Beth and me. I got in front next to Malcolm, and slid so close our thighs touched. Beth got in back with Davey Linder. Malcolm laid a hand on my thigh and said soft as silk, "I like your hair." He popped the cap on one of the bottles of beer, took a long swig and handed it to me. I smiled, took a drink as long as his and passed it to the back seat.

"Aaaaallllll right," Malcolm said. He gassed the car and we roared into the night leaving the other two boys. My hair was blowing free and wild in the wind.

Beth and I snuck out all summer long, meeting Malcolm and Davey. Sometimes we'd hear Roy in the background singing "Caro Mio Ben" or the

Nelson Eddy version of "Oh, Sweet Mystery of Life." His voice had changed and he was a baritone with notes so sweet and full, even I could almost cry.

The leaves were starting to turn and fall from the trees when I realized I was in trouble and would have to tell my mother. I waited till my father was off on a three-day train trip.

"I wanted better for you," she said. Then, "Who's the father?" Her voice was weak with anticipation, but her shoulders were square and her chin was high.

I swallowed hard and tried to match her gesture for gesture. "Malcolm Carter."

I could see a sigh of relief pass through her. "A good family," she said. "A big farm...a future there." She squared her shoulders again. "You'll get married."

"I don't want to marry Malcolm," I said. "I don't love him."

"He's a good-looking boy," my mother said. "A good family...they'll see he does the right thing...a decent match."

"I don't love him, Mother."

"A little late to be thinking of that, Rachel...Too damn late."

Malcolm and I were married before Halloween. I had to miss the last of my senior year and nobody but family came to the wedding. Roy sang Oh Promise Me and my mother cried. Malcolm and I had to live in my old room till the baby was born. The first few weeks of marriage were sweet and full of time and sexual discovery. There were sly looks from Roy in the mornings after Malcolm's more amorous nights but as my belly grew and the winter waded in, those nights disappeared. Malcolm took to sneaking out the bedroom window after I'd fallen asleep.

By April I was the size of Papa Carter's barn.

Roy came running home from school one day clutching a letter and yelling, "Mother, Mother, wait till you hear what's happened."

I inched my way down the stairs to find out what had him so excited.

"Mrs. Jones got a letter from Julliard today. They want to give me a scholarship to come and study voice."

My mother was scowling and wiping her hands on her long white apron as she came out of the kitchen. "Julliard?" she said. "Isn't that way off in New York City?"

"Yes, can you believe it?" Roy was almost jumping up and down. "Here read it," he said and thrust the letter into our mother's hands.

She swiped a hank of hair off her forehead and holding the letter in both hands, her knuckles white, she began to read.

Roy bounced from foot to foot. I labored to a chair and collapsed into it.

"They want to give me a four-year scholarship," he said. "To study voice with them. Mrs. Jones says with proper training I could be THE baritone of my generation."

He looked at me, wanting me to share his excitement.

"Yeah," I said. "And I could be the Queen of Sheba."

My mother's lips thinned and whitened as she read. I could see another family tragedy in those lips. When she was finished reading, she folded the letter carefully and handed it back to Roy. "You already have a beautiful voice and I need you here. You can't go to Julliard."

"A voice needs training, Mother. Education and practice to be strong, to develop range, to be perfect. I have to go."

"Tell Mrs. Jones, it's out of the question," she said.

"I will not," Roy said. "This is my chance to be someone, to get away from this stupid town." And he shoved the letter into his pocket and started out of the room. "I can be an opera star," he yelled. "Or the next Nelson Eddy and you can't stop me."

She straightened her spine, took off her apron, plopped a hat on her head and headed for the door.

"Mother, let him go," I said. "It's the only thing to do."

"I only want the best for both of you and look how you repay me," she said with a pointed look at my huge belly. "Just look at the thanks I get."

"Where are you going?" I asked.

"Over to the high school to have a word with Mrs. Jones."

My brother's dreams of Julliard died hard. He yelled angry words and pouted silently, withdrawing from my mother and her sick love. Still she refused to relent. She baked him pies and cooked his favorite food which he refused to eat. My mother sighed and took long walks bundled up against the chilly Indiana nights. It was a battle royal and I watched it unfold around the corners of my life.

"You can't stop me from leaving," he yelled.

"Mrs. Jones has informed them you won't be coming."

"I can be a star. Rich, famous, singing in the opera houses of the world."

"I need you here."

"You have father, Rachel, the new baby coming and the whole damned town of Muncie."

"I love you. I need you here."

Days of heavy silence followed the words until they erupted again. I thought he might actually go. I thought the family might fall in on itself and die. But it didn't.

My mother stayed strong, my father stayed gruff and Malcolm continued to climb out our bedroom window late at night while Julliard was lost.

It was early in May when my labor began and it wore on for hours in my room. The view outside my window went from dark to light and back to dark again while I sweated and grunted and swore at Malcolm and the world. The labor nearly tore me in two, but finally I pushed a baby boy into the world. He was ugly, misshapen and only lived two hours. Truth be told, I was glad to see him go.

As the small casket was lowered into the ground, Roy sang Amazing Grace and The Old Rugged Cross. Malcolm stood beside me, but we didn't touch and I never shed a tear.

Roy's lessons with Mrs. Jones continued but his songs were sadder now. I told my mother I wanted a divorce.

"There's not going to be a divorce in this family," she said.

"I don't love Malcolm," I yelled. "He doesn't love me either, Mother. He's been sneaking out for months now, seeing other women."

"He's from a good family, Rachel. A prosperous family. You could do worse."

"I don't love him. The baby is dead. There is no reason for us to stay married."

"It's out of the question," my mother said.

Looking back I can see I had many choices, but like my brother, I didn't know it then. My mother's iron will, her twisted love, her needs shaped our lives. Malcolm and I moved away but we stayed married for twenty-seven years till he died of the cancer and set me free. We had three more children and both of us continued to sneak out at night. Roy married, got a job, and continued his singing. On summer evenings his entire neighborhood stopped to listen as he sang That Lucky Old Sun, Some Enchanted Evening: the popular songs of the day. We stopped speaking to one another.

There was no famous baritone in our generation.

I'm thinking of my mother more as I lay dying...as the cancer grows in me, the same way I grew in her so long ago. I never forgave my mother for her twisted love that bent us and shaped our lives in such unexpected ways, nor do I yet today. She died years ago. Roy lives five minutes from her grave.

I wonder if he visits. I wonder if he still sings.

THE MAN WITH TWO FIRST NAMES

The neighborhood children called Herbert Albert the man with two first names. It was a good joke and he smiled and nodded when they did it. The children danced and laughed past his shoemaker's shop and sometimes stopped to chat or came into the shop with their parents to order shoes. He kept a jar of hard candy for them and their eyes sparkled with surprise and delight as the sweetness burst into their mouths between teeth and cheek.

Herbert thought of himself as a good man, a hard-working man, an honest man. He'd never hurt anyone. He loved the children, went to church on Sunday and sat with his wife and his own dark-haired brood in the seventh pew on the right.

The other six days of the week he went to his shoemaker's shop where he measured, cut and sewed shoes for the village and earned enough to keep his family in what it needed. Herbert loved the smell of new leather, dye and polish. He loved the thung, thung, thung of nails going through a new leather heel and the hot, oily smell of the stitching machine as he twirled and stitched a last. He appreciated the measured way the thread dipped into the leather and came out again. Herbert liked things orderly and right.

He loved the solitude of his work and the satisfaction of a well-made pair of shoes. He made boots for Stanford Jones and imagined them striding in the Jones' fine barns and fertile fields that grew corn like gold. He made sensible, sturdy shoes for Beatrice Smith and imagined them planted firmly on the polished floors of other matrons' parlors. He made dancing shoes for Charlotte West and imagined grand balls and the sweet warmth of Charlotte's feet as she waltzed with handsome suitors. His life was enriched by the lives of the people he made shoes for and by his imagination. His groin grew warm with the pleasures of his thoughts and he carried that home to his wife and life was good.

Herbert Albert's years passed. His own children grew big enough to move away. His wife thickened. Children still traipsed past his shop and he could see them from his workroom in the back. He nodded as they passed, but they seldom came into the shop and the jokes they shared excluded him rather than included him. The hard candy jar now held paper tags to attach to the shoes he re-soled, re-sewed, re-heeled and otherwise repaired. He seldom made new shoes these days as the villagers bought them ready made at Hartley's Department Store two blocks over.

There were still pleasant, dependable experiences in Herbert Albert's week, but if he were to tell the truth life wasn't what it used to be. The leather he worked on was stiffened by work or wear and lacked the buttery softness of something new and fine. He switched the heels on Putnam Lambert's boots to even out the wear and imagined Putnam working with his mules in the clay of his fields south of town. He resoled Mamie Cricket's oxfords worn thin with the miles she walked selling eggs and produce from her little cart and thought of her narrow, worried face. The only dancing shoes he saw were ready made and stiff, to be dyed for a color- coordinated wedding and never used again.

He thought about all of this in the back of his shop as he tapped and sewed and breathed in the air of other people's lives. And the seeds of his discontent grew into anxiety. He no longer felt secure in the back of his shop working on shoes, behind the counter exchanging pleasantries with the villagers, or even in his familiar pew on Sunday mornings. Even the dark, moist sex he shared with his wife on Tuesday and Friday failed to make him feel alive.

He put a bell on his door that tinkled to warn him when a customer came in and while he'd greet them at the counter with a smile, most times he didn't feel much like smiling.

Nothing stopped the years and Herbert's back curved from bending over his bench and his fingers grew stiff and sore as he did the little work that came his way. Fear became a deep, dark hole where Herbert lived, hurrying to the shop and home again, sometimes without ever lifting his hammer or turning on his stitching machine. And still the children walked by the shop. They were fresh-faced and new, the one thing that didn't change in a world that now wore plastic shoes and threw them away when things went wrong.

Herbert thought about this as he cowered in the back of his shop and day by day the children became his hope, his resurrection and his light. He watched them as they walked past his shoemaker's shop and thought about the sweet innocence of their faces that lasted year after year. Herbert wanted to laugh with them about something silly like his two first names or share the beauty of a measured stitch upon fine leather. He meant no harm and the sight of them calmed his fears.

He no longer knew the children's names, like he did in the old days but one little girl about six wore a pink ball cap with AMANDA spelled across the front in white letters. She walked past every day on her way to school and Herbert watched for her each afternoon on her way home. He began to depend on her and to imagine what her life was like outside the frame of his shop window. He imagined her warm and pink from her evening bath; with a studious frown doing homework after school; laughing with her friends and her life seemed good to him. His seemed better, too.

Herbert ordered fine pink leather and began to make a pair of small shoes. The softness of the leather warmed his knotted fingers and his soul. The purposeful progress of his stitching machine as the shoes went together calmed his fear so that he even hummed as he worked on his gift. He imagined Amanda's smile, he imagined her pleasure in the finely made slippers and he worked as he had when he was young, when life was fine.

The day the shoes were finished he put them in a box; sat on the bench in front of his shop and waited for Amanda on her way home from school. He called her name. Large eyes stared at him as if she didn't know him and finally he had to take her hand and lead her into the back of the shoe shop. She cried and screamed as if she didn't know that he meant her no harm, that he knew her well and that her entire life existed in his head. He told her he was the man with two first names. He laughed at the good joke, but Amanda cried. He slipped the perfect shoes on her feet, but Amanda kicked and tried to twist away. They fit perfectly and Herbert was pleased. He felt the heat of desire and spent it on Amanda. Her innocence was gone then and, of course, he couldn't let her go.

A TRIBUTE TO ARTHUR DIGGS
The Restmore Arms Nursing Home and Convolarium
Venice, Florida

January 10, 2010

Canter Phillips is sitting in the television lounge watching weather news from Ohio. "I don't miss the snow," he says to Arthur Diggs who fidgets on the green pleather couch, causing it to crackle like a litter of mice.

"Ehh?" Arthur says and tilts his head to one side aiming his hearing-aided ear more directly at Canter.

"The snow!" Canter yells. "I don't miss it!"

Arthur looks puzzled for a minute and then says, "Yeah, there's got to be a better show." He clutches the remote control in a gnarled and unsure hand, points it toward the set and changes the channel.

Work-out music and firm, sweating female bodies fill the screen. Keisha Krandalls' Body Works. It is a favorite among the early risers at The Restmore Arms.

"Look at those tits," Canter says. There is a wistful tone in his voice. "It's like waving filet mignon under a starving man's nose and not allowing him a bite."

Arthur nods. " Makes "Ole Blue" tingle with fond memories of my first wife, Norma Jean."

"Ole Blue?" Arthur raises an eyebrow, but keeps his eyes on Keisha and her exercising friends.

"Ole Blue is what I used to call my private member." Arthur laughs and his teeth clatter in his gummy mouth. "Named after my daddy's favorite hound. That dog could coax every she-hound in the county to back up to him. Half the pups in West Virginia looked like him for most of a decade." Arthur sighs. "I had some stray pups of my own back then. Norma Jean and half the women in Nitro pined for "Ole Blue" in the good old days." A single tear rolls down Arthur's craggy cheek. "I'd give anything for one more spree of "Ole Blue" running wild."

"The spirit's willing, but the flesh is weak," Carter says.

"Yeah." Arthur says and pokes a bony finger to change the channel back to the weather report.

"Why'd you do that?" Canter says.

"My heart can't take it. "Ole Blue" straining to lift his head and me living in a place with ten women for every man. Must be God's idea of a joke."

Canter eyes Arthur with disgust. "These saggy old broads would be no lark."

"Yeah, it's all pretty much the same in the dark," Arthur says as Donald Trump flashes on the screen. He is speaking earnestly about something. "Better than politics," Arthur says and clicks the remote to change the channel again.

Just then the new day nurse walks into the lounge. She is petite, young and cheerful. A long black pony tail bounces as she walks. Her name is Betty and she means to make a difference in the lives of the people she serves. "Time for morning meds, gentlemen." She is carrying a trayful of tiny, pleated white paper cups. She sorts out two and hands them to the men. "Breakfast is in ten minutes," she trills and watches while the men take their pills, then she turns on her toes and bounces out of the room, pony tail swaying in opposing action with her hips. The men exchange a horny glance, hoist themselves up and shuffle after her.

January 14, 2010

At 52, Dr. Marlon Harris still is a safe distance from becoming a resident at the Restmore Arms. Nevertheless, Tuesday is his day there - office hours from nine to noon when the Senile Olympics occur. At least that's how Dr. Harris thinks of them - old women on walkers, three pronged canes and wheel chairs racing for a spot on his morning schedule.

Dolores Beets is the winner this morning and wheels into the office first, eyeing the doctor with her head tilted at a coquettish angle. "It's time for my annual pap smear," she says.

He flips through her medical chart. "Wrong, Dolores. We just did one in November. The results were perfectly normal."

Her smile fades into the folds of her face. "I must have forgotten," she says. "It seems like longer. To tell the truth it seems like forever."

"Any other problems?" Dr. Harris asks.

Dolores starts on a tale about how long it's been since her son came for a visit. Dr. Harris glances at his watch and settles back into his chair to listen for three minutes, not a second more. To tell the truth, he likes the near-dead ones best, the ones who lay, curled into a fetal position for months on end. All he has to do is listen for a moment with his stethoscope, make a note or two on their chart and bill Medicare $28.50. He can examine twenty in an hour and to tell the truth, he needs the money. Two greedy ex-wives, three materialistic teenage children, an unemployed brother and an aging mother of his own have him financially strapped to the wall.

Dolores drones on. Dr. Harris glances at his watch and stands. Her time is up.

"Life isn't easy for anyone," he says as he escorts her out the door. The old ladies come and go in the order they arrived at the examining room. Most are hungry for attention, a swallow of the milk of human kindness, To tell the truth Dr. Harris has little of it to give. He is a man who, like his patients, wishes for a chance to go back and start over. But alas there is no going back, no fountain of youth, no cure for the indignities of aging for any of them. Dr. Harris has the added worry of a past-due payment on his Ferrari.

January 17, 2010

Arthur Diggs is sitting alone in front of the television set. He has a two-day growth of beard and his plaid robe sags against him. He can't sleep. The lights are low in the community room and reflections from an old black and white version of "The African Queen" have turned his face a ghostly pale.

"You feeling okay. Arthur?" Betty says. She has poked her head in the door on the way back to the nurse's desk after a call for assistance.

"Yeah," Arthur says. "Me and "Ole Blue are feeling a bit mopey."

Betty looks around the room for Arthur's companion. "Maybe you should see the doctor next week," she says. "Ask him to order you a sleeping pill."

Arthur sighs. "Lauren Bacall was a beautiful woman."

Betty's laughter tinkles in the room. She sits beside Arthur on the pleather couch. "All women are beautiful when you're lonely, Arthur." Betty sighs. "I'm lonely myself sometimes."

"Norma Jean was a beautiful woman."

"Norma Jean?" Betty says. "As in Marilyn Monroe?"

"Nah," Arthur says. "Norma Jean Diggs, my first wife."

"When did she die?" Betty places a comforting hand on his shoulder.

"She lied every time she opened her mouth. Left me for a man who drove a sixteen-wheeler back in '86."

"You've been single since 1986?"

"Off and on." Arthur says. "Married three more women, lived with a couple when that got to be the thing to do." Arthur's head dodders in the way of the very old. "But Norma Jean was always my favorite. Something about a young woman . . ." He eyes Betty, his head is still. "Like you."

Betty retracts her hand like Arthur's shoulder has caught fire. She stands and returns to the business of being a nurse. "I think you should talk to Dr. Harris. See if he'd order you a sleeping aid."

"Nah," Arthur says. "I'm going to watch the rest of the movie."

January 21, 2010

It is a quarter till noon and Arthur Diggs is hanging around the examination room door. He wants to see the doctor. He's getting up his courage when Betty walks by. "Glad you're going to see the doctor?" she says.

Arthur tilts his head to one side. "Eeehh?" he says.

"The doctor," she repeats her voice an octave deeper. "He'll give you something to help you sleep."

"Yeah." Arthur says. "I need to see the doctor."

Betty shakes her head and the pony tail swishes. "All right, Arthur. Good luck."

Alice Olsen is the last old lady to leave the examination room this morning and nobody else is waiting. Arthur watches as she labors up the hall with the centipede feet of her walker leading the way. She turns and smiles over her shoulder at Arthur before she inches around the corner and out of sight. Her cheeks are pink, her eyes glowing warmly.

Arthur walks into the examination room and finds Dr. Harris leaning over the sink scrubbing his hands as if he's preparing for surgery. Arthur shuffles his feet and takes a seat.

The doctor turns, drying his hands. "Well, well. A gentleman," he says. "What can I do for you?"

Arthur clears his throat, looks at his house-slippered feet. "Don't cotton to talking about such things to a man," he says as his face turns an embarrassed shade of red.

"I can't help you if you can't tell me what the problem is."

"I got an itch," Arthur says, not looking up.

"Eczema? Shingles?" the doctor says.

Arthur shakes his head. "Yeah. I been single way too long. I itch for a woman." Arthur lifts his head and looks the doctor in the eye. "Can you help me, Doc?" There is a note of pleading in his voice. "I'd give anything."

Doctor Harris crosses arms over his chest, leans back against the examining room sink. The three berries of a Las Vagas jackpot cha-ching into place in his brain. "Anything?"

Arthur nods.

"There is something," the doctor says, "But it's expensive and I have only a limited supply."

"Yeah, I'm willing to give it a try." Arthur says. He shuffles his feet. "How much?"

Doctor Harris doesn't hesitate. "Fifty dollars a treatment," he says. "And not covered by Medicare. I'd have to have cash."

February 12, 2010

The line outside Dr. Harris' office is shorter this morning, and it's mixed, both men and women of the Restmore Arms are waiting. There is quiet conversation among them. Word of Arthur's transformation has gotten around. The ladies have all combed their hair and put on a little make up. Arthur Diggs is first in line. He is shaved and a smile perks up the corners of his mouth.

"Hurt my back, Doc," Arthur says after he enters the examination room.

Dr. Harris eyes Arthur from under a raised eyebrow. "Don't you think you're overdoing this Arthur?"

"Screwing often as I can," Arthur says. "I just close my eyes and think of Betty. I feel like a middle-aged man again. Alice Olsen even chipped in for this week's treatment." Arthur pulls a wad of crumpled bills from his pocket and lays them on the examining table.

"How many pills you want this week?" the doctor asks.

"Valentine's Day is coming up," Arthur says. "Better give me six."

Dr. Harris opens his medical bag and pulls out a box of blue tablets. They are marked "Samples, Not for Resale". He counts out six and hands them to Arthur, scoops up the money on the examining table and stuffs it into the bag. "You want something for your back?" he asks Arthur.

"Nah," Arthur says. "I'll work the kinks out."

Dr. Harris sees all the waiting patients before eleven and takes off for an early lunch. He stows the medical bag in the trunk of his Ferrari (his payments are finally current) and roars off into Florida sunshine.

March 1, 2010

Betty can't help but notice the difference in the atmosphere at The Restmore Arms. Night calls are down 90%. Arthur Diggs is not sleeping in front of the television anymore. She does feel uneasy sometimes when he looks at her, but she knows she's making a difference in his life. She just isn't certain how she's doing it.

The old women are asking for more help with baths and trips to the beauty parlor. The old men are making more trips to the bank. Arthur has cashed in his railroad worker's annuity and is worried about how he'll pay this month's bill for his room at the Restmore Arms. Dr. Harris has upped the price of his special treatments to $100 each.

"I've been on a fixed income for twenty years," Arthur tells Canter. They are sitting in the atrium, where a Florida spring has sprung.

"The first rule of money management is never touch the principal," Canter says.

The whites of Arthur's eyes have a slight blue tinge. His bony fingers fidget with the lapels of his suit coat. There is a catsup stain on his shirt. "Ole Blue always had a weakness for the ladies," he says.

"How many of those treatments are you taking?" Canter asks.

Arthur stares into a bed of canna sprouts. The leaves are the bright red of fresh blood. "One every twelve hours," he says.

"That's fourteen hundred dollars a week."

"I never use on Sunday," Arthur says. "It's a day of rest and my daughter comes to visit.

Dolores Beets and Alice Olsen dodder past the men and smile. Alice has a flower in her hair and arches her spine suggestively. Her bones crack and pop like microwave popcorn.

Arthur starts to struggle to his feet to follow them.

"Never mind," Canter says. He lays a hand on Arthur's arm. "Let them pass."

"Yeah," Arthur says. "Ass is ass." He shakes loose from Arthur's grasp and goes after the women.

June 30, 2010

Arthur is curled into a fetal position, his eyes are closed, his face pale against the sheets. He doesn't move. Dolores Beets holds his pale hand in hers. She is singing Chattanooga Choo Choo in a wavering voice. Other women line the hall outside his room, waiting for a turn.

Betty and Doctor Harris enter making monthly rounds. They ask Dolores to wait outside, then roll Arthur onto his back. He is sunken and thin, a shadow in the bed, except for the spot where the sheet tents over "Ole Blue" that still stands proud and tall. Dr. Harris shakes his head and sighs, presses his stethoscope to Arthur's chest. Betty gives the doctor a blushing smile. "Nothing to be embarrassed about," he says.

Betty nods and takes Arthur's chart, tucks it under her arm. "To tell the truth, I find him oddly erotic."

Dr. Harris smiles softly. "I have something I could give you for that."

"In tribute to Arthur Diggs?"

"He was one of my best patients. I feel like I owe him something special."

Betty nods. "He was a favorite of mine, too." she says. "He ran out of money, you know and we were going to have to put him out of the Restmore Arms."

The doctor makes a tsk, tsk sound. "Thank God for Lyndon Johnson and Medicare."

Betty stares into the doctor's eyes. "Oh, no," she says. "It's not like that. I never imagined this could happen, but the women pool their money and every month they pay his bill. It's the most amazing thing." Her eyes sparkle with tears and the doctor's do, too.

"Just when you believe the world has no good left in it, something like this comes along and makes everything right," he says.

"Yes," Betty says. She feels good. Like Dr. Harris could make a difference in her life. He puts an arm around her shoulder and silently escorts her out of the room, past the old women waiting in the hall. They all take their turn with Arthur, and occasionally Ole Blue twitches under the covers, bringing a smile to the comatose Arthur's lips.

WHEN MAMA DIED

The family fell apart when Mama died. Nobody ever called me smart but after she was gone even I could see she was the glue that had held us all together. Daddy was standing by her bed holding her hand as she passed. His feet shuffled with embarrassment as her last breath came and went. My three sisters and I were standing around the bed holding each other's hands and crying like our mama just died. I have to say I was sobbing much as anyone and hated to see her go. Daddy was pale as Mama and might have been mistaken for the one leaving this mortal life as he folded Mama's limp hand across her dead, flat chest, so I was surprised when eight weeks later he was married to Betty Sue Carson who was only twenty-nine and had a half-black son she'd brought home in her womb from a single year at college eight years earlier. And a year after that I was sitting in the Clarksburg jail accused of killing her.

"Some education that girl got," Mama had said when Betty Sue came home. Betty Sue developed a reputation around town and my friend Curtis and I both had a go at her before the baby was born. "The damage is done," Betty Sue said to all comers. I can't help wondering what Mama would have had to say about Betty moving into Daddy's life like she did. She moved right into Mama's house and Daddy's bed. I think the child took my old room but I can't say for sure.

I saw daddy at the hardware store two weeks after the wedding and his step had a new spring. His beard was neatly trimmed and his clothes were pressed nice and crisp. He looked like a younger version of himself.

He saw me, too, but didn't stop to chat or ask how I was. He just nodded in my direction and stepped on down the aisle, like I was some acquaintance and not his only son.

I wasn't sure how I felt or what I ought to do about my new step-mom. I decided to stop by the house and introduce myself though she knew well enough who I was.

She smiled when she opened the door. "Malcome," she said, "Your daddy's gone but you come on in and talk to me." The child stood behind her with eyes big as softballs and just as blank. She led me into the kitchen and offered me a piece of pie fresh out of the oven and a glass of cold buttermilk, which is my favorite thing in all the world. She opened the refrigerator, bent over, shoving her butt out into the room in an exaggerated way and pulled a waxed milk container out.

"Naw, I better be going," was all I could stutter out. "Just wanted to say hi to my daddy since I was passing by."

Betty Sue smiled and nodded as she put the buttermilk back into the refrigerator which looked full and prosperous like I hadn't seen it since the cancer first grabbed my mama. "You still staying over at Curtis's house?" she asked.

I'd been staying with Curtis over two years now and the whole town of Clarksburg knew that but I guess she was a bit flustered by my being there, back in my mama's house. The place looked familiar but clean and fresh with the blinds rolled up and the sun streaming in windows that sparkled with a fresh cleaning.

She didn't urge me to stay and the child never came out from behind her as she walked me to the door.

"I'll tell Walter you stopped by," she said as she wiped her hands on the cloth slung over her shoulder. Her hip was thrust forward and she showed her teeth beneath a mischievous grin.

"A man needs a wife," my best friend Curtis said when I told him about my visit. "Wouldn't hurt you none to have one of your own," he said. "And a son or two to go with her. Something to think about besides your daddy and that wife of his."

"I never needed a wife when my mama was alive," I said.

Curtis grinned and got a look that made me want to wipe it off his face with a fist.

Curtis and I had been friends since we were born so he knew there was bad stuff stewing in me that needed taking care of.

Mama used to help me with the bad feelings when they reared up inside of me. Darkies she always called them. "You got the darkies today Malcome?" she'd ask and I'd know I was going to feel better soon. She could tease the meanness out of a snake and she was a lot better than that when it came to me.

I could have used Mama's teasing when I let myself think about that Betty Sue, her butt, her mischievous grin, her boy and my daddy living snug as a hutch of bunnies in my mama's house.

My three sisters all were married and I visited each one of them in turn looking for an easing of the hurt that was inside me. They were astonished at what our daddy had done but they had husbands and babies and were no help to me.

"Get over it, Malcome," they all said.

"I don't like it either but there's nothing to be done," they echoed.

"Mama's dead and in the ground."

It made me sad, it made me cry. It made me mad. It gave me the Darkies like I never had 'em before. I tried to carry on. Curtis and I both worked at the filling station. I never missed a day, not one single day in two whole years except the day my mama died. Curtis missed that day, too.

I could fix anything on a car and people brought their cars in just to have me look at them. Betty Sue and her boy started dropping by. She'd sit there in the driver's seat and call me over to the window where only I could see inside.

"How are you today Malcome?" she'd ask and lift her skirts to show her knees. The boy in the back seat couldn't see anything and neither could anyone at the station. It was just between Betty Sue and me. I got sort of a sick feeling in my stomach to think of my daddy's wife lifting her skirts for me. I also felt a heat pass through me that just wasn't right. It all made my mama's death and my daddy's needs seem like a really bad joke. A bad joke Betty Sue was trying to pull on me. I didn't tell anyone what Betty Sue was doing, not even Curtis, but her boy knew and I knew. He'd look at me with those huge eyes from the back seat of the car and we sort of gelled in the process.

I thought about my mama and how she loved my daddy and all us kids. I thought about the way she'd cook our favorite meals when we came home to visit and how she looked after my daddy. It seemed all for nothing when Betty Sue moved into her spot. The more I thought about it the more it seemed Betty Sue made my mama's entire life disappear. I thought Betty Sue's boy felt that way too, though he didn't know my mama from the man in the moon. I know my mama never showed her knees to the likes of me.

When Betty Sue drove into my filling station I'd get real busy under somebody's car and refuse to walk out to see her. Curtis would raise his eyebrows and get that grin on his face because he knew I was avoiding Betty Sue and he could only guess why. I didn't care. I'd just keep on about my business till she drove off with her boy in the back seat, and I wouldn't let Curtis see I was bothered. At least I tried.

It was a crisp fall day when Betty Sue drove my daddy's big old car into the station and laid on the horn till I came out. Curtis went out first and Betty Sue said she had to talk to me. I went out.

She smiled at me in that "making a suggestion" way she had and said, "Your daddy's having a baby, Malcome" I felt myself go hot and cold all at the same time. I looked at her boy in the back seat and he was looking back with those round old eyes and he was smiling, too.

She rubbed her belly, threw back her head and laughed as she gassed that car and fish tailed out of the station lot. Curtis was standing at the door of the station wiping his hands on a rag watching the whole thing as it happened.

"She's gonna have a baby," I told Curtis when I got enough spit back into my throat to speak. He shook his head and we both went back to work.

I watched Betty Sue flirt around Clarksburg for all the month of September and half of October. We passed the first anniversary of the day my mama died. And then one day I saw my daddy at the hardware store buying a chain for the tractor. Time was going backwards for him and he looked even younger than the last time I'd seen him.

"Malcome, boy. How you doing?" he said and he clapped one of his big rough hands on my shoulder. "Did you hear you're having a new baby brother or sister?" He beamed with the news.

"No child of Betty Sue Carson is kin to me," I said and shook my daddy's hand off my shoulder.

"Betty Sue's my wife now," I heard him say as I stomped out of the store. "She's your step-mother and the baby she's carrying is going to be your brother or sister and nothing you say or do will ever change that."

I didn't look back but the Darkies were on me for the next week so bad that I missed two days of work. Curtis tried to help but there was nothing anybody could do. I just kept to myself and tried to think what Mama would want me to do.

It was Wednesday morning when Betty Sue pulled into the lot. She revved the engine of the car and honked the horn. Curtis looked at me over the hood of Bart Speigel's Pontiac to see what I was going to do. "Don't go out there, Malcome," he said.

But I went anyway and when I walked up to the window of the car she asked, "Want to stop by for a little lunch?" She asked with that smile she had. "The damage is already done."

I knew she was pulling her old tricks and this time it was my daddy who was the goat. I reached into the car and pinched off the air that went to her brain. I squeezed and squeezed   all the time looking into the eyes of Betty Sue's only son and when he realized I wasn't letting his mama loose he started screaming and didn't stop till Curtis helped put me into the back seat of the Clarksburg cruiser that carted me off to jail.

They found me guilty at the trial and sent me off to prison, but Betty Sue was gone out of my daddy's house and I think Mama would have liked that.

RIDING THE TIGER

I didn't grow up wanting to join the circus, but when I had the very good luck to meet Antonio, it became my life. Antonio was a juggler, and a good one if I do say so myself. He could juggle thirty electric hula hoops at one time and when they turned off all the lights, it looked like a herd of multicolored lightning bugs were doing laps at the speed of sound. It was pure magic.

Antonio was so handsome I thought I would die when he walked into the Arthur Treacher's Fish and Chips where I was passing time at the drive thru window till I decided what I really wanted to do with my life. He had midnight hair swept back into a duck's ass and a crooked grin like Elvis. In fact that's who I thought it was, though I didn't believe those Elvis sightings we were always reading about in the Inquirer. He strutted, more than walked, moving his body with the control and authority of a man who lived well in it. I was handing an order out the window when I first saw him. The order was going to the firehouse and it was a big one, but I just stood there with my mouth hanging open and a hot oily bag of fish flapping in the breeze while I looked Antonio over.

He noticed me watching him, winked one of his black gypsy eyes and I thought I would wet my pants. A man seldom affects me like that, but Antonio was a seldom kind of guy. I let loose of the bag of fish without ever looking back out the window, pulled off my apron and shouted "Emergency Break" toward the kitchen where the manager was busy training a new girl on the fryer. I could hear the firemen's horn blasting at the window as I walked away.

My eyes never left Antonio's as I approached him.

"I believe the fairies have got me," Antonio said. He smiled and I took his arm. We walked out arm in arm and I became part of the circus that very day.

On performance nights the circus is about magic, sequins and wide-eyed children. It's about the exotic, the death defying, the suspension of regular life. Riding the tiger circus people call it. Antonio became all those things to me. He taught me to bow with exaggerated movement and to hold my arm out towards him like he had just invented the wheel when he pulled Foxy, his cashmere bunny out of a hat. His mother made me a suit of golden sequins and white net that turned me into a fairy princess on the nights we gave a show. Antonio said the entire point of having a pretty girl on stage was to distract the crowd's eyes from him and he taught me just those moments when I needed to call attention to myself and away from him. He taught me to handle the hula hoops with a flourish and to toss him his juggling balls so there was never a slip or a drop. He taught me not to pull away from the flaming torches and sabers that he twirled and tossed about like they were no more threatening than marshmallows. And he taught me that when the spotlights went out there was real life to be lived and love with the same excitement as riding the tiger.

Traveling with a circus is very hard work. There are animals to be fed and miles to be covered, tents to be raised and tickets to be sold, even food to be prepared and laundry to be done. After a show was completed the trucks were packed up and gotten ready to roll again. Usually we slept a few hours before actually pulling out of town so we started the new leg of the journey refreshed. There were sweat and tears and mud in a circus life and I embraced it all. I worked harder than anyone until those moments late at night, after the show, when Antonio and I could be alone. Our lovemaking was mingled with the memory of a thousand people holding their collective breath, the gentle stamping of the horse's hooves as they settled into their trailers and the blood red smell of the meat the tigers ate. It was the kind of love a woman would gladly die for.

Because I was with Antonio I was accepted by the other performers but it was clear he was a one-way ticket and that without him as my mentor I'd be dropped by the side of the road wherever we happened to be. City or countryside, it wouldn't matter. I had no real family talent like the bareback riders or the trapeze artists who were trained to play their roles from birth. I only joined the circus to be with Antonio and many were not happy to welcome me.

Antonio usually followed the bareback riders in the third ring while the tigers' cage was set up in rings one and two. The tent went dark and all eyes were on Antonio and his hula hoops while the low roars and the clank of metal against metal happened under cover of darkness. It sounded like a night in the African jungle and only added to the intensity of Antonio's act. At least that is what Antonio said and what I believed.

"Are you ever afraid?" I asked him and he laughed. "Fear is for the rubes," he said "It comes with the ticket."

I confessed to Antonio that I was afraid of the tigers. He began taking me round for their feeding and introduced me to Carlos their trainer who had me stand beside the cage while they meticulously ate the meat he gave them. Carlos and Antonio would go inside the cage when the tigers had been fed and the cats actually rolled on their backs to have their bellies rubbed as if they were giant cheshires. "Man is the only carnivore who kills when he is not hungry," Carlos told me. "A satisfied tiger is made from paper. A hungry tiger is a killer." His eyes glistened as he spoke. "Besides I double check every lock and will never forget to secure the beasts." As the weeks went by I began to believe him and my fear subsided.

Chantelle was the leader of the bareback riders and she tried her best to wring the last bit of juice from the audience before Antonio and I went into the ring. His mother told me she was jealous of our love and this was her way of getting back.

"Were they lovers?" I asked.

His mother shrugged. "Antonio is not the sort of man to be without a woman." She refused to say more and I was left to believe what I wished.

Every performance was new and exciting. It was as intimate and intense as making love. Antonio and I waited in the shadows while the horses. carrying their sparkling girls, thundered past us breathing hard and spraying sweat. In the next two rings the roar of the tigers rumbled menacingly. Antonio's signal to enter the ring was a smack on my behind that stung just enough to please me. We were a single unit bonded by the rhythm of our souls. I'd rush into the ring ahead of him and strike a pose until he entered and began to twirl his hoops waiting for the spotlight to find us and flash on. I could feel the tingle left by Antonio's slap, smell the tangy fragrance that hung in the air for the first few minutes after the horses' exit. I could hear the electric hum of the hoops in the dark and the gasp of the crowd as the lights flashed on. Some nights it was enough to make me climax.

Antonio and I had been together just over four months when the accidents began to happen.

First it was little things like stolen hula hoops and torches. Then Foxy, Antonio's angora bunny, took sick and died. Antonio's mother fell and broke her ankle when she slipped on some oil that had carelessly been allowed to leak onto the steps of her travel trailer . "Bad luck," Antonio said and shook his head. His eyes glowed darkly and he turned his back to me when he went to sleep. The chorus was repeated by other members of the crew and they looked at me whenever I walked by and talked behind their hands.

It was October and we were headed back to Florida where the circus wintered when the final tragedy struck. We had played Valdosta, Georgia, and loaded up the show for the final time of the season. The crew and the performers were excited knowing the long winter break was just ahead and I was looking forward to the long nights of winter to rekindle the love Antonio and I had lost.

The crew was napping for a while before we pulled out of Valdosta and I lay snuggled against Antonio's back while he snored softly into the quiet. Outside I could hear the shuffling of feet on gravel and the whisper of sharp words. I rolled away from Antonio and peeked out the window next to our bunk. Chantelle was standing by the window looking back at me. Two figures in black were running away from our little caravan. Then I heard the roar of the tigers and the sound of Carlos' shouts.

"The tigers are loose. The tigers are loose," he shouted.

Chantelle struck the exaggerated pose of one who had just invented the wheel before she turned and ran toward the sound of Carlos' voice.

I caressed Antonio back and said, "The tigers are loose."

He sat straight up in our bunk and turned his gypsy eyes on me. "Bad luck," he hissed and shook himself free of my hand.

FISHING NAKED

It was the weekend of the bass fishing championship of Ohioana County and I was a bass fishing fool. So were most of the other guys who lined the bar at the Knotty Pine Grill where we hung out four nights out of seven in a regular week and every night that the championship was happening.

"The problem with fishing naked is you can't wipe the worm goo on your pants," someone said.

I looked to see who was speaking and it was a woman with blond hair and a low-cut peasant blouse. You know the kind with a string that pulls it up over the shoulders. and gathers the fabric gently for such a nice effect. It gives a lot of skin to the sunshine. The woman was young. She was pretty and she was filling out the peasant blouse in a very pleasing way.

John and I had been hopping bars since 4:30 pm when the first twelve-hour fishing shift ended. We watched as the boats raced to get back to the weigh station on time and as the fish got weighed in. It had been a long day and we were ready to either have some supper and sober up or go all the way to drunk and disorderly. It was the second night of the tournament and we were doing our best to be good hosts to the people in town for the event. I'm not normally a lady killer of a guy and am as likely to slink into a corner and watch as I am to put myself into the center of a provocative situation..

I don't know what came over me. It might have been the blond hair, the peasant blouse or it might have been that John was standing there beside me breathing into my ear. But I lifted the Coors bottle to my lips and drained it. "Baby, I'd fish naked with you any day," I said.

John poked me in the ribs as I spoke. The guys at the bar snickered and sort of leaned back giving the blond and me some room to negotiate. Little spurts of laughter escaped here and there.

That woman leaned into the bar and looked down at me. She didn't say a word but then she didn't have to. She stuck a finger into the air and motioned for me to move on down the bar toward her. Well, I was happy to oblige and John ordered us up a couple more beers and one for the lady.

"What's your name?" she said after she had pulled a hefty chug from the cold bottle.

"You can call me Big Bass," I said.

She had turquoise blue eyes, a most arresting shade, and they sparkled when she spoke.

"Big bass, I've got my poles in the car and I think we'll be sorry if we don't rise to the occasion that has presented itself."

The guys sitting along the bar were looking at one another and guffawing. They were sure I'd back off from the challenge. I was shy, but I was a fishing fool. "What's your name?" I asked.

"Dolly Vardin," she said with a smile.

"Dolly, you're on," I said.

She leaned her head back and I could see the muscles of her throat working as she drained the bottle John had bought her. "No boats, no clothes and no tackle boxes. Worms on bare hooks," she said.

"Primitive," I said. "I can do that."

"Two-hour time limit," she said. "And the most weight at the end wins."

I nodded and money started to change hands along the line as betting on the outcome got underway.

"Winner calls the shots for the rest of the evening," she said. Cat calls and whistles rose above the general hum of the bar.

"Meet you at the end of the dock in a half hour," she said.

I checked my watch. It was 8:30 so the contest would get underway at 9. John said we ought to have another beer before we left and I said no. I wanted to get to the car and get my gear together.

I left John at the bar, got my stuff and staggered as best I could to the dock. Dolly had a crowd gathered round her by the time I got to the end of the dock. The good old boys were standing around her three deep. She had to shoo them away so I could get close.

"You boys got to give us some room," she said. "I'm not stripping down for the world, just for Big Bass over here and whoever it is that's going to be the beer runner." A chorus of volunteers stepped forward and she pointed at two guys who smiled and wiggled thinking they had won some great prize. "The rest of you get back to shore," she said. The others left with a lot of noisy complaints.

She sent the first beer runner off back to the Knotty Pine with an order and she checked her watch. She looked over at me.

Okay, Big Bass," she said. "Time to take it all off."

I was having second thought but couldn't figure out a way to back out now so I took off my clothes and folded them into a pile by my feet.

Dolly did the same and the crowd on the shore quieted down while she did it. It was plain to all of us that Dolly was a very special girl with or without the peasant blouse. "Bait up," she said. I pulled a nightcrawler out and globbed it onto the hook in a tantalizing display. I tossed the hook into the water and began to reel it back towards me with a up and down motion . Dolly did the same and then she came close and wiped a big gob of worm goo up and down my leg. "See what I meant," she said.

"You were right," I said and went on to catch eight pound, ten ounces of bass off the end of that pier before the two hours expired.

Dolly beat me, of course, but I didn't mind at all.

FINAL TIME AROUND

Walter Allison was in love. Not for the first time in his life, but perhaps for the last. Her name was Marcella Brooks and she had the smile of an angel and twinkling blue eyes that laughed when she looked at him. She was young, maybe too young for a man his age but Walter believed that in the case of love exceptions sometimes had to be made. He also had learned some things in his life and he knew enough to keep them to himself. That's why he and Marcella met secretly for the first few months of their courtship. It wasn't always easy with the eagle eyes that were on alert twenty-four hours a day at the Forever Young Assisted Living Facility where the two of them met.

Walter would be ninety-six on his next birthday and Marcella wasn't even into her eighties yet, just a few years older than his children he'd be reminded later. But they both remembered things most everybody else only knew about from reading history books. They liked the same music and they could share a joke. Through the days and nights of secret rendezvous they let their relationship develop slowly, like a soup that just got better as it simmered.

"I thought I'd die myself when Clara died," Walter said. "I'd met her in Sunday School when we were both in second grade. It was 1914," He said, "and she was the prettiest girl I'd ever seen."

"I met my Herman in church, too," Marcella said. "At a hayride when we were in high school. We got married in my mother's parlor three weeks after Pearl Harbor and before he went off to fight The War." Tears flooded her eyes even after all these years. "Poor Herman, he never came back."

"Clara could bake a loaf of bread so sweet and warm it would make a grown man cry." Walter's voice was wistful, his eyes were sad. "We were married for sixty years, Clara and I. We still have four children living and one who died in Viet Nam. He was our baby who came as a surprise to both of us when Clara was forty-three."

"I regret not having children," Marcella said. "I'd have liked being a mother."

"Like everything else in life, children are a blessing and a curse."

And so they shared their history and their dreams. They sat together in the commons room and watched Masterpiece Theater, fingers secretly entwined so no one else could see. And eventually, late at night when the staff was small, and after much coaxing and cajoling, Walter would sneak into Marcella's room and climb into her bed. Love was no less lovely the final time around.

"There have been some others since Clara died," Walter said after one particularly passionate session. Marcella had squeaked and squealed with the ardor of the night. Walter had become fearful the night staff would hear and come to investigate.

"I understand," Marcella said. "A man like you . . ." she let the sentence trail off as she planted a trail of kisses down his cheek.

"...needs a woman," Walter finished for her. Marcella sighed and laid her head on Walter's shoulder. It fit just right.

Marcella stared up at the ceiling then turned her face toward Walter. "The only man I ever had was Herman." Marcella blushed. "Till now, of course. I am a Catholic girl," she whispered. "We held out for marriage."

"All those years?" Walter was astounded but it made him treasure more the gift she'd given him.

And so their love deepened and time meandered on.

It was fall, getting on towards Thanksgiving. The trees had done their autumnal stunts and the gorgeous leaves had fallen to the ground. Walter took it as a sign that must be heeded. He crept into Marcella's room and found her there reclining in her bed...waiting. He pulled a chair up close and with hands shaking, voice croaking with anticipation he blurted out, "Marcella, I think I love you. Will you marry me?"

"I'd be proud to be your wife," Marcella said and so the stage was set.

Walter leaned over the bed and kissed Marcella passionately on the lips. "You've made me the happiest man on earth," he said and started to climb into bed with her to seal the bargain.

Marcella pulled the blanket to her chin and held it there. "I'm sorry, Walter, but a wedding changes everything. You mean the world to me and getting married means a lot, I want it all to be perfect. Pure and unsullied by demon lust."

Walter was dumbfounded but he loved Marcella and he wanted her to be happy.

He kissed her chastely on the cheek and made his night time way back to his own narrow bed. The next morning he paid Joe the maintenance man and van driver at Forever Young to drive him to the jewelry store to buy Marcella a ring. He picked out a half carat with an emerald on either side. Marcella was born in May and she loved her birthstone. There was no keeping a secret once the ring was purchased. Joe was a reliable man who was working hard to make ends meet and raise five children, but he was not to be trusted with this kind of a secret.

So Walter gave the ring to Marcella in the commons room after Masterpiece Theater and in full view of Abbie Kingory who was deaf as a tree and nearly blind as well. It was as private as most things got at the Forever Young Assisted

Living Facility. "When do you think we should get married," he asked.

"The weekend between Christmas and New Years," Marcella said. "That will give your children time to adjust to the idea and me time to plan the wedding." She held her hand out as far as it would go, spread her fingers in the classic halt gesture and admired her engagement ring by turning her hand from side to side. "It's beautiful," she said. Walter smiled and held her other hand.

Walter called his oldest son Don and asked him to stop by for a visit the next day. They sat in the commons room away from the television set where a group of women were watching Dr. Phil. When he told Don what he planned to do, you'd have thought he'd confessed to murder.

"Married?" Don said with a dumb look on his face. "What about Mom?"

"Your mother was the love of my life and nothing will ever change that, Don, but she's been dead since 1991."

It's ludicrous to have children over the age of seventy and a fiancé only eight years older but it was what Walter was dealing with and he did his best. "She's young enough to be my sister," Don said.

"Well, erm, yes she is but she's also certainly old enough to be my wife."

"She's a gold digger, dad. I bet she's marrying you for your money."

"You haven't even met her yet. How could you possibly think that?" Walter narrowed his eyes and asked, "You're not worried about your inheritance are you?" Don didn't answer but his face turned red and he bit his lower lip.

"Have you discussed this with the others?" Don asked.

"Not yet," Walter said. "You're the eldest. I brought it to you first. And you need to understand, I'm not asking permission, I'm informing you of my plans.

"You're ninety-six years old, Dad. What could you possibly want with a wife?" Don leaned back into the couch and crossed his arms over his chest. He put a small pout in his lips that Walter recognized from his childhood.

"The regular things. Love, companionship, the warmth of a bed that's shared."

"It's disgusting for a man your age to even be talking about sex," Don said.

Walter shrugged. "You asked the question but I really don't think it's any of your business."

Walter led Don down the hall to where Marcella was waiting to meet him. Marcella was charming and low key. "I've heard so much about you, Don," she said. She extended her hand in an offer of friendship but Don just noticed the ring and turned the hand to examine it closely.

"Gold digger" he muttered, turned on his heel and left the room. Walter and Marcella stood dumbly and watched his back retreat. Walter reached over and took Marcella's offended hand. He raised it to his lips and kissed the palm. "This might take a while longer than we thought," he said.

Walter paid Joe, the maintenance man, handsomely to take Marcella shopping.

There were several trips before she found a dress for the wedding. It was the palest pink silk that complimented her snowy white hair. The night nurse had her mother take up the hem an inch and Marcella ordered roses in shades of pink that scanned the spectrum from light to dark. She wanted the wedding to be memorable. She wanted things to be nice and while the planning went on she continued to deny Walter the comforts of her bed. "I am a Catholic girl," she'd say and Walter would sit beside her bed, holding her hand till it was time to return to his own room before the morning change of shift.

Walter's children formed a coalition and objected to the marriage. Don was the leader. They all snubbed Marcella when they came to visit their father and the visits increased by three fold after they learned of his wedding plans. Christmas came and went. The New Year began with Walter more in love and frustrated physically and emotionally by the turn his life had taken. Marcella set Valentine's Day as her new potential wedding day. The bounce went out of Walter's step but his jaw was set firm.

"I won't let a child of mine dictate my life," Walter said to Marcella one night.

"It's best if they approve," Marcella said. "I'll be happy to sign a pre-nup agreement, Walter. I don't want or need your money. I've got money of my own."

"I know that," Walter said. He let his fingers trail up and down Marcella's arm till all her little hairs were standing up on end. "It's just the principle of the thing." He looked at Marcella, he struggled to his feet, leaned over and kissed her on the cheek.

"Let's make love," he said. He pleaded with his eyes.

"Things are so different now," Marcella said. "I just can't till the knot is tied."

So Walter called his lawyer and they spent many hours behind the closed doors of the conference room at the Forever Young assisted living facility. Eventually Walter came forth with an agreement. His shoulders slumped and his ears turned pink when he stood by Marcella's side as she signed it. Walter had his attorney standing by as he made a big production of showing it to his children.

"Iron clad," he told Don. "Everything is iron clad."

Don was less than pleased but after a long hesitation he nodded. All concerned gave circumstantial blessings to the marriage and the wedding went forth as Marcella had planned. It was memorable and it was beautiful. The residents of the assisted living facility attended and Walter and Marcella moved into a double room. The first week they even took their meals there.

Love was lovely, it was warm, it was sweet the final time around. The spirits of the entire place lifted as the newlyweds celebrated and as the long hard back of the winter was broken and began to give way to spring. It was May, a week past Marcella's eightieth birthday, when Walter fell ill. Marcella sat by the bed and held his hand while he hovered between life and death. She climbed in with him and held him tight. His children checked in on a daily basis and found them this way more than once.

"Disgusting," Don said and beat a hasty retreat each time.

"Promise me you'll go to the reading of my will," Walter said on one of his last good days.

"Don't die on me, Walter," Marcella said. "This is getting to be a pattern in my life." She clutched his hand and held it to her heart.

"I love you, Marcella, but I think I'm going to have to go." He coughed and squeezed her hand. "Promise me," he said.

Marcella nodded. "I promise," she said. Tears filtered through her lashes and she sat beside him till the end.

Joe, the maintenance man, drove Marcella to the attorney's office on the day the will was read. They sat isolated on the far side of the room from Walter and Clara's children. Marcella clutched a hanky in her fist and sat proud and tall in a hostile environment. She thought Walter would be pleased.

The attorney cleared his throat and began. "We are here for the reading of the Last Will and Testament of Walter J. Allison. He was father, husband, friend to each of us and he was of sound mind until the day he died."

Walter's children shifted in their seats, Marcella clutched Joe's hand and the attorney went on. "Walter executed a new will that excluded Marcella at the same time he had me draw up the pre-nupt agreement that his children insisted on. The new will also excludes you children."

Don jumped to his feet. He glared at Marcella. "You are responsible for this," he said.

"Sit down and shut up, Don," the attorney said. "These are his wishes, let there be no mistake about that.

"He left his considerable holdings, his land, his money, his mineral rights, his stocks and bonds, to Joe the maintenance man who supported his marriage to

Marcella from the beginning."

"And he never told a soul," Marcella said. "Not even me." She reached over and shook Joe's hand.

Tears were falling from Don's reddened eyes.

"Ironclad," the attorney said. "Walter made sure it was ironclad."

WIDOW'S WALK

Red queen on black king. Black two on red trey. The electronic slap of the cards was a lullaby that soothed Janis Carson as she sat playing computer solitaire. It was 4 am central standard time. Light from the screen illuminated her face and turned her naked skin blue before it sunk into shadows on the walls surrounding her. It's what she did instead of sleep since Jack died. She liked the orderly way the cards lined up on the screen, the everlasting number of games available with the click of her mouse and the excited music that announced a victory now and then.

"Be careful what you wish for," her mother always said. Janis hated to admit her mother was right about anything, but she was right about that. Janis had wished Jack dead and now he was. Dead as he would ever be and she was alone. As alone as she'd ever been. Her mother was dead now, too, but her words still rung in Janis's ears. The slap of the cards drowned out the words for a while.

"Give yourself time," her friends said, but they clung to the arms of their husbands in a predatory way, like Janis might try to snatch them away. Skinny-legged old men with slack in their pants and dandruff on their shoulders. Men too much like Jack to have any appeal.

The Golden Years some young fool has called them. Janis couldn't see anything the least bit golden about them. The golden years had been back in the day when Janis was firm and fertile. When she still had all the things the world adored. She'd used them up and now they were gone, just like Jack. She didn't miss Jack but she'd love to have one more time around the track as a thirty-something or even -God-grant-me-the-serenity-to-accept-the-things-I-cannot-change-, sixty-something. Those were the days and Janis knew it.

She moved the final ace and the cards counted themselves down onto the pile at the bottom of the screen. The tinny orchestra played its TAAA-DAAA congratulating her on her victory. "Oh God," she said, "I wish I had another chance."

The TAAA-DAAA turned into a funky little ragtime tune and the screen took on a reddish glow.

Dialogue boxes appeared and Janis blinked to see if she was imagining things.

The letters of her name appeared on the screen J -A-N-I-S?

Janis looked around the room. She was still alone and she knew she hadn't logged on. She was just playing a game all alone in the privacy of her bedroom where the computer sat on a table she'd moved in from the garage after Jack died. The bed was rumpled and unoccupied, the door was open and casting a narrow shaft of light into the hall.

Another message appeared. "Janis, It's me, God."

"It is not." she said.

"Type into the dialogue boxes," was the next message on the screen.

She typed. "It is not."

"You think God can't talk to you over the Internet?"

"If he could, he wouldn't ask me to type into the dialogue box." she typed. "He could read my mind."

She heard a wicked giggle and looked again around the room.

"You'll never see me," a voice said at the same time the words appeared on the screen. The voice was liquid and soothing.

"What do you want?" Janis said.

"You're wishing for another chance?"

She thought a moment. "You aren't God," she typed. "He doesn't offer deals like this."

Again that wicked giggle filled the air behind her. "You're right," showed on the screen.

"So who are you?"

"Guess."

"I can't."

"I'm a little devil."

"Right," Janis typed. "I should have known. I'm not giving up my soul."

"Tsk tsk. Do you think we're all a bunch of one trick ponies?" and the giggle echoed behind her again.

"How should I know."

"What you really want is love, right? Love that is better, sweeter, kinder and more considerate than what you got from poor dead Jack."

"I wished him dead, you know?'

"Of course, I know. Why do you think he died?"

Janis thought about what that might mean but didn't type anything on the screen.

"Cat got your fingers?" showed in the box.

Still Janis typed nothing.

"Your wish is my command."

"Yes," she typed slowly. "I want love."

"Another time around will cost your soul but I can get you love for half of that."

"What's half my soul," Janis typed.

"Could be one of your children. Could be one of your parents. Or it could be something else."

"Something else?"

"You know. A mutually negotiated treat," the little devil typed.

"I don't like the sound of that."

"It's a reasonable choice," he typed. "Jack is here with me. He'd like to have some input."

"Jack's there with you?

"As we speak."

"In Hell?"

"Hmmm, I don't think I said that did I, Janis?"

"Where are you then?"

"We're out here in cyberspace. You know."

"Jack?" Janis called out. "Say something."

"Hi, hony. How u doin?" appeared in the dialogue box.

"It is you, isn't it?"

"Uf corse, it is. Did you think the little guy was lyin?"

"You're not mad that I wished you dead."

"Uf corse not. I wished myself ded many times." Laughter echoed in Janis's bedroom.

"Do you think I should do it?"

"Yes, itz a sure fire way to git what you want. Itz how I got to be talkin to u."

"What did you give up?"

"I cudnt tell u that, hony. Itz aginst the rules."

Janis was silent. Her hands rested in her lap and still words kept appearing in the dialogue box on the screen. They were words she might have uttered and Jack attributed them to her.

"I'm all alone," the words said.

"Well, duh?, hony. U go around wishin ur lovin husband dead and then feel sory 4 urself becus ur alon?"

"I'd like a little love before I die?"

"My firey little friend told u how to git it."

"I'm not selling my soul."

"It only hurtz the first few seconds," Jack typed onto the screen. Then there was more laughter in the room. "I swear."

"That's not me talking, Jack . It isn't me."

"Don't wory hony, Let me take care of everything. That's what love is all about anyway. Bein takin car uf, Iznt that what u always said?"

"You never loved me, Jack. You were always too busy loving yourself."

There was silence in the room. Janis checked the screen to see if any of Jack's fractured words were appearing on the screen. The screen was blank. A chill passed up Janis's spine. A quivering chill that reached into her heart.

"Jack? Where did you go?" Janis typed.

There was no answer, there were no words in the dialogue box, no wicked laughter in her bedroom.

The computer had returned to the excited music that said she'd matched all the cards in yet another game of solitaire.

BILLY BARROW'S GHOST

Dot eyes her mother's rhinestone shoes as Ethel slips them on. "You're going to a funeral, not a prom," she says.

"It never hurts to put your best foot forward," Ethel says. She lifts her foot and admires the shoe. "There are bound to be restless spirits around after a sudden death. Billy married me four times. Sparkly shoes got him every time. Dot raises an eyebrow as her mother goes on. "If his spirit is hanging around I want him to know I don't harbor any hard feelings that we weren't officially married when he took a mind to blow his brains out."

"It wasn't your fault," Dot says.

"I know that. It was that harpy, Doreen, made him do it. He never should have moved in with her and Rube when I threw him out."

"Rube is his only son. Where else would he go?"

"The Motel Six?" Ethel says. "Curtis Longerman's couch? Anywhere but Doreen's house." Ethel stomps a jeweled foot. "I don't know how Rube stands her."

Dot shrugs. No point trying to talk sense to her mother, even under the best of circumstances. Today is not the best of circumstances. Today they were burying Billy Barrows who has dispatched himself from this world standing on a coffee table in his daughter-in-law's newly decorated rumpus room. A revenge of sorts against a woman who was never pleased about anything.

Dot heard the details when Sheriff Shorty La Mont stopped by the diner for coffee. "He shot himself through the chin with his WWII revolver. You never saw such a mess. Bits of brain, skull and that fiery red hair all over Doreen's new furniture. She liked to never stop screaming." The sheriff shook his head at the memory. "Poor Billy laying in a heap, his toes still looped over the edge of the coffee table and Doreen running from chair to chair with her dust buster."

Dot hadn't shared these details with her mother, but the casket was closed "due to circumstances" and she'd gone to Walmart with Ethel to buy a frame for the photo they set on the lid for the viewing. As if anybody could forget what Billy looked like with his only son and spitting image still up and moving around.

Dot sighs. "Okay, Mom. Wear the rhinestones, but I think the only restless spirit you're likely to connect with is Doreen's and it's going to be mean."

Ethel looks in the mirror, fluffs her bottle-blond hair. "Doreen never gave two hoots about Billy...Rube either, if you want my opinion." Ethel catches Dot's eye in the mirror. "We both know she'd never had that new rumpus room without Billy's rent money."

"She blames you the room is ruined and there's no money to clean it up."

"Shows how stupid she is. Would I have gone to all the trouble of another divorce? Would I have missed out on the widow's benefits if I'd thought he'd go and kill himself?

Billy promised he'd look after me, no matter what and he's not left me a cent. Not one red cent...and after all we've meant to one another." Ethel adjusts the narrow belt on her black dress. "I think he'll show up today, if only to haunt Doreen a bit more." She turns sideways, checks herself in the mirror. "How do I look?"

"You look fine," Dot says. "But you don't really expect Billy's ghost to show up at the funeral do you?"

"I do," Ethel says. She smiles and her eyes sparkle. "I saw him slipping through the hedge last night. Like he used to when he'd been out late gambling and raising hell with Curtis. He looked guilty, like something's keeping him from resting easy."

"Did you run out to talk to him?"

"No, I just watched. Everybody knows you can't catch a ghost."

Dot shrugs again. "Billy's dead. He's laid out and waiting over at Shaw's Mortuary. He wasn't slipping through the hedge last night. Besides he's dead by choice. Not much in that to be restless about." Dot shakes her head. "Sure wish he'd left a note though. It would have cleared up a lot of questions for all of us."

"Sure would have, but Billy always liked to leave people guessing," Ethel turns back to the mirror, purses her lips and applies a generous coat of gloss with her little finger. "I saw him with my own eyes, and I'd know Billy Barrows anywhere."

Dot and Ethel enter Shaw's Mortuary on either side of Curtis Longerman, Billy's best friend and occasional companion. Curtis wears tattered jeans and a black leather jacket. Shoulder length gray hair is pulled back with a beaded band that cuts across his forehead and trails feathers down his back.

"Thanks for waiting for us, Curtis," Ethel says. "Billy always said you were a good man to have at his back."

"I promised Billy I'd look after you and Rube right after your second divorce. He never took it back and neither did I."

Ethel smiles at Curtis as they walk through the chapel doors. Sheriff Shorty LaMont stands at the door in full uniform. Ethel nods at him and threads her way through the crowd to walk past Billy's coffin, though there is nothing to see but the wood-framed picture. Ethel reaches out and touches the photo. Tears fill her eyes. Dot hands her a tissue, Curtis shifts from foot to foot while Doreen harumphs from the family row. Rube dabs tears from his eyes but doesn't move to offer comfort to his father's most frequent and recent wife

Ethel eyes the family's row of seats. All are taken. Misty-eyed she leads Dot and Curtis to empty chairs near the back of the small chapel. Curtis nods greeting to those friends of his and Billy's who have made it to the service.

The tense silence is broken by shuffling feet, stifled coughs and the squeaking of wooden folding chairs as bodies shift until one of the Shaw boys turns on the taped organ music. Finally a shiny-suited preacher stands and begins the service. Ethel recognizes him as a cousin of Doreen's who is likely to be under her influence.

"Billy Barrows was a sinner," he begins and then launches into a list of Billy's sins and sinning companions that shocks even Ethel. The sermon is pure hellfire and brimstone from the word go, offers no words of comfort to the bereaved and is in fact so inflammatory that a few of Billy's mourners leave even before their names get mentioned.

Ethel can see Doreen's shoulders square and her head tilt toward Heaven as the minister moves along in his sermon. Ethel crosses her arms, grits her teeth and holds her seat, determined not to let Doreen run her out of Billy's funeral. That's when she feels a cool breeze against her cheek and hears Billy's voice plain as day inside her head. "Don't that woman beat all?" he says. "Can't even let a man be buried in peace."

"I knew you'd come," Ethel says.

"I noticed the shoes," he says. "I thought blowing my brains out all over the rumpus room would shut Doreen up but it's only made her meaner. I know I said I'd always take care of you but Doreen's made me change my will."

Ethel looks from side to side, wonders if anyone else can hear the voice. Curtis snakes a sinewy arm around her shoulders and Dot stares straight ahead. She can't be sure. "What will? You didn't even leave a note."

"Rube is going to make a run for it. Let him go." Billy's voice says inside her head.

When the service ends, Doreen turns and scans what is left of the crowd. She wears a look of complete and utter triumph. She pokes Rube and he turns too. He looks tired. He sees Ethel and nods. She nods back before Doreen grabs his arm and pulls him toward the family exit at the front of the chapel. Ethel smiles when he salutes with his free hand in what can only be interpreted as a farewell gesture before Doreen pulls him outside.

"That Doreen's got the sensibilities of a skunk's ass," Sheriff La Mont says to no one in particular and the Shaw boys begin to herd the remaining mourners out of the chapel for the ride to the cemetery.

"Never could understand what Rube saw in Doreen," Dot says as she hustles her mother toward their car. "She's as mean spirited as a cobra. No wonder Billy killed himself."

"It's going to haunt her," Ethel says. "You wait and see."

"I'm almost sorry Billy's ghost didn't show up," Dot says. "I'd like to see him get her after she had that preacher crucify every friend he ever had."

"Will you ride with us?" Ethel calls to Curtis as she gets in the car.

"No," he says. "I'd better ride m'bike. I got a feeling I may need it." He fingers hair back behind his ear and walks toward his motorcycle.

"You afraid Doreen'll try to run us off the road?" Dot asks.

"Wouldn't put anything past her after this," Ethel says. "It'll be weeks before people stop talking about it, unless of course, something bigger happens."

"I guess you wore those shoes for nothing."

Ethel just smiles and doesn't say anything.

The Shaw boys have moved outside. Doreen is seated like the Queen of Sheba in the black funeral limousine, Rube is alone in Billy's old El Camino behind the limo and Sheriff LA Mont has his blue lights flashing ready to lead the procession to Billy's final resting place.

Dot and her mother sit and watch. Ethel is surprised to see Rube in his father's truck and even more surprised that Doreen has allowed it in the procession. She realizes something is going to happen...something Doreen isn't controlling.

Cars file by with their little funeral flags waving and Dot finally pulls in near the end of the line with Curtis on his Harley right behind. Just as she is ready to leave the lot one of the Shaw boys taps on her window. She rolls it down.

"Rube wanted your mother to have this," he says and hands the picture to Dot.

"I told you Rube and I were the only ones who cared about Billy." Ethel takes the picture and holds it to her breasts. That's when she notices the envelope taped to the back. It is addressed to her in Billy's cramped handwriting and the seal is torn open.

If you're reading this, I must be dead. Peace is what I'm looking for and that Doreen wouldn't give me a moment of it. Don't know how Rube stands her.

There's 20 years of poker winnings, $10,000, buried in the back yard at the base of the sour apple tree. It's yours.

Love,
Billy

"What is it?" Dot asks. "An apology? An explanation from Rube?"

"No," she said. "It's Billy's ghost in action."

Ethel crumples the note and shakes her head. She cranes her neck to see the front of the funeral procession. When Shorty LaMont's blue lights turn right with the hearse and the limo right behind, she sees Rube in Billy's rusty old El Camino turn left.

Dot sees this, too. She looks at her mother. "Should I follow him?"

"No," Ethel says. but she sticks an arm out the window and motions Curtis to follow Rube and he wings off left after the El Camino. "But he's going to need a good man at his back when Doreen gets word he's gone." She throws back her head and laughs all the way to the cemetery. She thinks somewhere Billy's ghost is laughing too.

THE CASE OF ERNIE LORD

Ernie Lord's Tailor Shop occupies the only building left on its block. Once part of a bustling commercial district, it is now surrounded by gravel parking lots and sticks up like the last worn tooth in an old man's jaw. It blocks the development of a plot of nearly prime city real estate. Samson is a blue and gold macaw, who spends his time on a perch in one dingy window of the shop greeting the handful of customers who still come to Ernie for tailoring - mostly alterations. The shop and the macaw are the only things that still matter in Ernie Lord's confused life.

It is morning and Samson is squawking, impatient for Ernie to deliver his breakfast through the curtain that separates his private quarters from the shop. Ernie is late this morning (this is happening more often these days) and droopy-pant boys are already trailing past the window on their way to school or whatever other trouble the day holds for them. A pair of them have stopped to knuckle the window and yell "Shad-up," at Samson. He spins on his perch, spikes his feathers and fixes them with a one-eyed stare. "French fries," he squawks.

"I'm coming," Ernie calls from the back of the shop. "Quiet down, Samson. You trying to wake the dead?" He shuffles toward the front window, a cup of mixed seeds and nuts in one arthritic hand. The boys tap on the window again. Ernie sees them and yells, "Get out of here, you hoodlums. Leave us alone."

The boys laugh. One hooks his thumbs through the front loops of his pants, lowers them in front, leans back and pees copiously on the window. The other tosses a handful of gravel at the wet spot. The dust sticks leaving a gray trail down the glass.

"Hoodlums," Ernie yells. He drops the seeds, hurries towards the window, and tries to jerk open the front door. It is still locked. "Dirty little heathens," he yells. The boys run off down the street, laughing and slapping one another on the back.

"Damn criminals," Ernie shouts after them. "That's the last straw," he says to Samson. "Having to clean their gritty pee off my windows." He brushes the spilled seeds back into the cup, dumps them into Samson's feeder, and removes the water dish. He pours the leftover water into a scraggly plant that sits by the door and shuffles back through the curtain.

By the time Ernie returns with fresh water and a key to unlock the front door, Samson is grinding sunflower seeds and dropping shells on the floor of the paper-lined display window. He stops to watch Ernie with his unblinking eye and squawks, "French fries".

"Not today," Ernie says. "It's only Tuesday. No French fries on Tuesday," He reaches over, scratches the bird's forehead. The bird leans into the affectionate gesture before he goes back to his breakfast.

Samson is sixty-two and Ernie is eighty-four. They've been together since 1956 when boys didn't pee on shop windows and this section of Main Street had no parking lots. When the ladies walking by wore hats, gloves and suits with lapels that were properly interfaced, not synthetics held together with Velcro. Ernie remembers the old days better than he does yesterday. He remembers he'd meant to find a wife and have some children but the time for that crept past him and when he noticed, it was too late.

Ernie still stitches with an enviable fineness but lately customers show up to reclaim work he hasn't completed yet and Amos Carter had to be buried in his pajamas when Ernie misplaced the jacket his widow brought in for final repairs. Ernie found the jacket three days after the burial, stuffed behind some dusty bolts of pelum. He is embarrassed by his failures.

Ernie is a stubborn man who could have sold out to Ponti Renewal Projects last year when the other neighbors did but he and Samson never wanted to be anywhere else. They were comfortable in the shop. They had their routines. Daniel Ponti was impatient for Ernie to die and Ernie wasn't doing him any favors. In the meantime he and Samson have to bear the indignities of the neighborhood's young hoodlums.

"Have to call the police," Ernie says to Samson. It is his only defense.

Ernie is hosing off the window when they arrive two hours later. They pull the cruiser up to the curb on the wrong side of the street and climb out, shoulders reared back, pelvises shoved forward in the confident, relaxed posture of the young. They smile as they approach in their ready-made city blues.

"Took you long enough," Ernie says as he adjusts the hose nozzle till just a trickle of water dribbles out. He pulls himself tall as he speaks to the younger men.

"Your seventh call already this month," the taller one says. His shiny name tag identifies him as Snider. The other is Jones.

"They peed on my window," Ernie says gesturing with the hand that holds the hose.

"Looks like you've destroyed the evidence," Jones says. He lays a hand on Ernie's shoulder and Ernie shrugs it off. Samson sits on the other side of the glass swiveling his head, watching first one and then the other.

"They're criminals," Ernie says. "A blight on innocent citizens."

"C'mon, Ernie, they're kids," Snider says. "Attracted to the parrot, no doubt." He taps on the glass. Samson flaps his wings and squawks. His feathers separate and ruffle across his shoulders.

Ernie's eyes narrow. "What parrot?" he says. "Samson is a blue and gold macaw. He came from South America. One of the last of the native born."

"An illegal alien?" Jones says. "We might have to run him in."

Snider reaches out to tap on the window again and Ernie lops the hose end across his knuckles. "That's what the hoodlums do," Ernie says. "It upsets him."

"Sorry," Snider says. He grins at Jones. "Guess we better take our report before he calls the cops on US."

The cops question Ernie and scribble notes. They hold the report out on a clip board for Ernie's shaky signature. "We'll come as often as you call," Snider says. "But why don't you try making peace with these kids? Ask them in to meet the bird. Make friends?"

"Like making friends with the devil," Ernie says. "Not likely," and he shakes his head.

"Suit yourself," Snider says. He looks at the single building, the surrounding parking lots. "I can see you're a stubborn man, but if I were you, I'd think about taking the bird and going south. Soak up some rays, ogle bikinis." he pokes Jones in the ribs and they head for the cruiser laughing.

Samson squawks and ruffles his feathers. Ernie adjusts the hose to full squirt and grumbles, "Cops are as bad as the criminals these days."

Lunch is saltines and a bowl of tepid split pea soup which Ernie eats sitting at the jumbled desk where he works on his accounts. He has cleaned the front window on both sides and spread clean paper under Samson's perch. Samson paces along the bar and squawks, "French fries," as Ernie has his lunch.

"Leave it alone, Samson," Ernie says. "You have to wait till Wednesday for your treat."

The bird flaps his wings and ruffles the feathers down his back in agitation. "Gilligan," he squawks.

"You're confused," Ernie says. He breaks a corner off a saltine, shuffles to the window and holds it out for Samson. He takes the bit of cracker in his beak and then lets it fall to the floor. "French fries - Gilligan," he says.

"You're getting senile," Ernie says. He flips the switch on a small television at Samson's eye level and steps back. "See for yourself."

Black and white horizontal lines flip down the screen and then stand up to show a snowy Professor speaking earnestly to Mary Anne while the Skipper looks on. Samson settles his feathers, tilts his head to one side and watches.

Ernie shakes his head, runs knotty fingers through his thinning white hair, "Must have changed the schedule," he says and goes back to the desk. Samson swivels his head watching the small grainy screen. "Hello," he says when Gilligan enters the scene. "Hello, Gilligan."

Ernie smiles and settles back into eating his soup.

The bell on the door jingles and two men enter the shop. One is tall and wears a handsome custom-made suit. The other is muscular and tough looking in ratty jeans and a Grateful Dead tee shirt.

Ernie looks up from his soup. "Can I help you?" he says. They are at his desk before he can rise.

"Ernie Lord?" the taller one says.

Ernie doesn't speak. The two men stare at him, not in the simple opposite-eyed way Samson does, but in a way that looked into the deep places where Ernie hides his fear.

"We have a message for you from Mr. Ponti," the tee shirted one says. He advances on Ernie who tips the desk chair getting up.

"It's time to sell," the suited one says. "Get yourself a condo in Florida...move to Arizona...die...Mr. Ponti doesn't care...but he wants this building."

"It's mine," Ernie says. "I won't be bullied . . ."

The tee shirted man grabs Ernie by the collar, lifts him off his feet and drops him on the overturned chair. The legs crumble under Ernie's weight.

"Hello," Samson squawks from his perch.

The men are startled, look around the shop. Ernie groans from the floor.

The suit laughs. "It's the bird," he says.

The other man relaxes and grins, sheepishly. "Oh,"

Ernie begins to hoist himself up from the floor with the edge of the desk. "Criminals," he says. "Nothing but a bunch of hoodlums."

The muscular man starts for Ernie. "No," the other man says. "We delivered our message, now it's up to him."

Ernie is standing now, but he is shaky.

"When Mr. Ponti's lawyer stops in, sign the papers," the suit says.

"Or we'll be back," the other one says.

Samson squawks, "French fries," as they walk past. The suit shakes his head. The tee shirt punches Samson in the head and he falls off the perch to the paper lined floor, out cold.

The two men look back at Ernie. "Sign the papers," the suit says. "Or you are next."

The men walk out the door laughing.

Ernie is breathless, his heart pounding when he gets to Samson. He runs his fingers under the slack feathers, finds no blood but a lump is raising on the bird's head. Ernie sits on the window ledge rubbing Samson's feathers, all his energy is concentrated on the bird. Tears well up in his eyes. "I'll kill them for this," he says.

Samson's wing rustles against the newspaper lining the window. He struggles to his feet and squawks half-heartedly.

"Thank goodness," Ernie says. "I thought you were dead." The bird is unsteady on his feet and Ernie smooths the feathers on his shoulders and back. Samson turns his head from side to side, looking around the shop. "It's okay," Ernie says. "They're gone now and I'll be ready for them if they come back." Ernie holds out his hand, Samson wraps his toes around the wrist and Ernie lifts him to his perch.

Samson's tail feathers are bent in two directions and tiny bits of downy under feathers fly off when he flaps his wings, but he shakes his head, wraps his feet around the bar and holds his perch. Ernie watches him closely, scratches his forehead till Samson ruffles his feathers in response.

"You're okay," Ernie says. "You are okay, old boy." Then he makes for the curtain with a purposeful stride. In his private room, the drapes are still pulled against the day and the bed is rumpled. He rummages in the closet and pulls out a leather box. He carries it to the bed, sits and opens it. Inside is a Ruger he brought home from World War II. There is a small rust spot on the barrel but it still smells sharply of gun oil. Ernie rubs a finger over the rust spot and his mind goes back to the sights and sounds of war...the danger and the fear. He will protect himself and Samson.

Ernie carries a chair from the back to the desk and kicks the pieces of the broken chair behind a counter. His cold bowl of split pea soup still sits atop the desk. He pushes it aside and sits with the Ruger until he nods off. Samson is on his perch watching horizontal lines flip down the television screen. Boys approach on their way home from school. They stop at the window and peer inside. Samson squawks at the sight of them and Ernie stands up tall and brave as he's ever been. He lifts the tarnished Ruger and fires.

The boy's eyes widen in surprise as the glass shatters and bullets pepper the air. Samson flaps his wings and squawks as Ernie hurries to the door.

"I warned you," he says. "I told you to leave us alone." One boy is hit and blood makes a red trail down the sidewalk. The other looks at the gun in Ernie's wobbly hand before turning tail and running for help.

EMT's put the injured boy on a stretcher. With sirens blaring and stray gravel spinning up from their tires, they carry him off for medical care.

Snider cuffs Ernie's hands behind his back while Jones drops the gun into a plastic evidence bag with gloved fingers.

"What about Samson?" Ernie asks. His eyes are glazed, his thin hair poking madly in several directions.

"I don't know," Snider says.

"The windows broken," Ernie says. "We can't leave him at the mercy of the streets."

Jones and Snider nod. The three men stand limp-armed and uncertain watching the bird through the broken glass. His feathers are iridescent blue and gold, a blot of beauty against the gray building.

"I guess we should call the SPCA," Snider says.

Tears fill Ernie's eyes. "Can we drive him there?"

"It's not procedure," Jones says.

Snider looks from Ernie to the macaw and back to Jones. "Screw procedure," he says and with Ernie's guidance, the cops transfer Samson from his perch to the back of the cruiser.

Snider and Jones get in front.

Samson flaps his wings and squawks, "French fries".

"I told you, Samson, no French fries till Wednesday." Ernie says.

The cop's eyes meet. They shake their heads. "Today IS Wednesday," Snider says.

Ernie's forehead wrinkles in confusion. "It's Wednesday?" he says. "Well, could we stop and pick up some fries on our way?"

CHAS AND BABY

Death has a way of slowing things down, giving you time to think, trying to see the error of your ways. I know this because I'm dead, stuck hovering above a world that is going on without me. I had a notion death could be more than the end, but I never expected this.

The last thing I remember, Chas and I were screaming down I-77 on his Harley. Chas was torqued on some Meth he had scored the night before and I was hanging on for dear life, my teeth dug into his shoulder like a tick. The red-gold glow of a late summer dawn was peeking over the Appalachian Mountains like a chalk outline around a body but I didn't notice. I was high on life, high on Chas, high on love, adventure and the moment I was in.

Chas always called me Baby, but my name is really Maureen. I left the name and everything else about my white-bread life behind the night I met Chas at a Grateful Dead concert in Buckeye Lake, Ohio back in 1992. I never looked back, till now.

Chas rounded a curve and ran his bike right up the ass of a General Diaper Service Truck starting it's early morning run. I could hear Chas yelling, "BAAAAABBBBYYYY" as I flew off the back of the bike and through the early morning air. There were diapers floating everywhere, like seagulls out on a Sunday afternoon and me landing on my head with a nasty thud. Fini, kaput, kibosh. The fat lady was singing her little heart out and life as I had known it was over.

I could see Chas leaning over me, tears streaming down his cheeks, not a scratch on him, except his shoulder where I'd bit out a hunk that was still stuck in my mouth. The diaper truck driver was hopping around like a herd of baby goats, grabbing diapers from the air and stuffing them in a bag. It was funny and I had the urge to laugh till I zeroed in on my body laying there with its nose against its shoulder at an angle that was all wrong. I hesitated and I think that's what got me stuck, which I still am today, looking on.

That's what I've been doing since it happened and may be doing literally forever unless I can figure something out. I haven't seen any long bright tunnels, dead relatives, or God, or Mohammed. No Jerry Garcia either for what that might matter. I'm on my own with it all. It isn't bad really. Sort of float-y and being everywhere at once and knowing things you never thought of before. Now there's the rub.

I went to the concert on a bet with three girls from the office. We decided around the water cooler it was the thing to do. We all worked hard, long boring hours and owed ourselves a bit of adventure before it got too late. I tucked my two babies into bed that night and Bruce Jr., who was only two, cried because he didn't recognize me in my tie-dyed costume. I hugged him tight, brushed back his silken hair and kissed his forehead before I walked out of the room, leaving him to sniffle himself to sleep.

Bruce was in the living room of our little house watching an Adam 12 re-run on TV. I kissed him, too. He didn't look at me. "I won't wait up," he said.

"OK, Hon." I smiled, feeling invisible which had been happening a lot lately. I loved Bruce in a beige sort of way. Had loved him since tenth grade and marrying him just seemed the thing to do after we both graduated from high school and he got a job with the bank. Bruce Jr. and his big sister Kayla came along easily enough. Perhaps too easily for me to appreciate them properly.

"Don't take up with any bikers," he called after me. I know he meant it as a joke but it turned out to be a prophecy.

Nita, Rita and Ruby were the girls from the office. Not one of us was over thirty. We giggled like teenagers, packed into Rita's beat up old Toyota for the twenty-mile trip to Buckeye Lake. Ruby had brought a bottle of wine and we passed it around as we neared the concert site. It heightened the anticipation of the adventure ahead. The chance we were taking, even being there among the Dead Heads.

We could see them from the freeway, spread across the hill. Spray painted Volkswagen busses and long-haired types in tie-dye, just like us. The excitement mounted in the Toyota and something surged in me. I thought it was some primal thing, more real and urgent than my real life called for.

Rita threaded her Toyota through the crowd and pulled to a stop next to a day glow green van where long-haired people were cooking sausages on a hibachi, drinking beer and smoking dope. I could smell the sweetness on the air. We passed around the bottle of wine again and tumbled out of the car into a world of rebellious spirits, the legacy of the if-it-feels-good-do-it days. A world I'd only seen in movies and television newsreels. I tingled with excitement.

Love hung in the air. Well, love and sex. Couplings occurred here and there. Nobody took any special notice. In this place it was the most natural thing in the world. Holy almost. And with the dusk came the music and rowdy laughter. We breathed in the second-hand smoke and Ruby and I floated off from Nita and Rita. They are not twins, by the way. Just friends with rhyming names. they stopped to share a joint with some folks with gray in their hair.

I first saw Chas among a group of people on bikes, most, but not all of them were Harleys. He was straddling the bike like he had just arrived. His legs were long enough to reach the ground and I noticed first that he was wearing snake skin boots. Gray ones.

They were the same shade as his eyes which met mine boldly. I tore myself away when Ruby called my name, but I could feel the heat of those eyes following me. They pulled me back again and again as the music and the darkness gathered the crowd in and made us one.

It was Ruby pushed me toward him. "Go on, Maureen," she said. "We came to have a little fun."

And so I went.

"Hi, Baby," he said and from that day forth, it was my name. He slung a leg over the bike and put his arm around my shoulders. I snuggled into him like he was my long-lost soul. He was muscled like a fighting dog and smelled like licorice. I have always loved licorice. He introduced me around the group and each person smiled and spoke to me like I was their new best friend. I wanted to be.

We sat side by side listening to the band. Chas braided wildflowers into my hair. He held my hand, breathed warmly onto a shoulder he had bared with his teeth and when I lay back on the grass, showed me Orion's Belt and Aquila, the eagle among the stars.

The crowd mellowed out and so did the band. The music was harmonious and soft by the time Chas and I made love. The grass was cool on my back, but warmed up when he moved inside me like he was making a nest. The faces of my children faded as he awakened unborn feelings in me and took me places Bruce would never know.

Before it was over, I knew I could never go back, could never go home. I had found a new home and by the time the girls came looking for me the stars were cold in the sky and Chas and I were halfway to Pennsylvania. Chas wanted to show me the little house on the Ohio River where he was born and more than anything else in the world, I wanted to see it. My hair was loose, the flowers had been lost to the wind and Bruce, Bruce Jr. and Kayla were a restless memory.

I didn't think. I worked hard at not remembering and once passing through Orlando, I wrote a card to the kids and almost sent it home. Chas shook his head, tore the paper into confetti and sent it sailing in the air. Chas and I loved and laughed and dwelt among the stars. My love for him was red and green and gold.

Three years passed and the investigation into my disappearance had been scaled back by the time I realized it was occurring. Chas and I were in a motel outside of Santa Fe when a segment of "Unsolved Mysteries" came on the television and there was Bruce, Bruce Jr. in his arms, Kayla by his side, making a plea for my return. He looked older, sadder and Kayla seemed taller by a head. "Nobody knows what happened to Maureen Albertson," Robert Stack said in his most serious voice. "If you have any information, please call Unsolved Mysteries today."

"It's me," I said to Chas. "I'm on television."

"You gonna call Bruce?" he asked and looked at me with those eyes. His hands were warm on me. I shook my head and he flipped the channel to ESPN and a skateboard final. Later, while he slept, I called Ruby.

"I'm alive," I said. "Tell Bruce to stop looking for me. I'm not coming home."

I heard the sharp intake of her breath. I heard the confusion in her voice. "Maureen??? Maureen? Is that really you? Bruce has been like a crazy man. Your children miss you."

"They'll get over it." I said. The sharp edge in my own voice surprised me.

"Everything has changed," she said. "We should never have gone to that concert."

"It was the best day of my life to that point and every day since has been better."

"We all thought you'd been kidnapped and it was our fault."

"I'm happy," I said. "I'm not coming home. Tell Bruce."

It was abrupt, it was unfeeling, it wasn't like the old me at all and I didn't realize how much I'd changed till after I was dead.

I am knowing everything now. I can feel it all.

Bruce's confusion and fear when I didn't come home, the bite of a million tears my children cried, the guilt of Rita and Nita.

Everything I caused.

I feel it all the time, while I'm floaty and all alone.

While I watch the world go on.

Bruce and Ruby got married and my children call her mom. They are beautiful to watch. I miss them now and would give nearly anything to feel them small again and in my arms.

Chas found another woman, too and I see all that. He calls her Baby and braids flowers in her hair.

Sometimes I cry.

JOSEF THE FABULIST

Josef was tall and Teutonic with those transparent blue eyes you can almost see through. I was on a business trip to Indianapolis and into the vodka martini's like I grew up in Siberia. I had also been living celibate after a particularly nasty break up with a computer guru who was moving off to California. Josef looked really good to me. Good enough that I decided it was time to end my long dry spell.

"You have beautiful blue eyes," I said and couldn't detect a hint of a slur in my voice.

"The better to see you with," He said and smiled a crooked smile.

"Little Red Riding Hood was a German fable."

"Most of the best ones are. They were first published in 1852, you know." He flicked a finger at my martini glass. "Would you like another?"

I nodded and cuddled into my bar stool like there would be no tomorrow. Josef snaked an arm around my waist and pulled me toward him. I let myself be pulled.

"The Brother's Grimm?"

"Yes," he said "and their stories were bloody enough to scare the bejesus out of most self respecting children back in the day." I love it when men say back in the day. It means they have a few years on them and a bit of knowledge they might be willing to spread around.

"I guess Walt Disney cleaned them up for modern kids."

"Somebody had to do it." he said

Our drinks came and I took the first sip of the new martini. It was ice cold and crisp. Good. I said, "Yummm," and set the glass back on the bar. Josef played with the condensation on the side of his Coors bottle.

"Are you a book expert?" I asked.

"More a fabulist," he said.

"And that would be...what?" I asked taking another sip of my martini.

"I'm an expert on stories, like Clarissa Pinkus Estes. Fairy tales are some of the very best stories."

I looked into Josef's blue eyes, thought about how long the computer nerd had been gone and cooed, "I just love fairy tales."

"I have a copy of an early edition of the Brother's Grimm at my apartment," he said. "I'd like to show it to you."

I licked my lips and took another sip. "Josef, I would just love to see something like that."

It wasn't the worst decision of my life, but it was close. He was as cool in bed as his eyes looked in the soft light of the bar. He couldn't find the book of fairy tales which I doubt ever existed and he had me back inside the bar in an hour. I thought I might wait a while before I tried again.

It was six weeks later when I experienced the burning when I went to the bathroom. I visited my gynecologist and he said, "Herpes, your friend for life." He gave me some pills he said would help and told me I needed to inform any future lovers and take precautions for their sake. He also said I should question anyone I had been with recently in case the one who infected me didn't know he was contagious.

I knew that meant Josef and a trip back to Indianapolis, two hundred miles to the north. I went on my first free week-end. Josef was there, sitting at precisely the same spot along the bar.

I climbed up beside him and bought myself a ginger ale.

"Josef," I said. "Read any good books lately?"

Those pale blue eyes looked me over and he smiled. "Your name has escaped me," he said.

"Louise," I said. "I was in here six weeks ago and you gave me something."

Josef looked puzzled. He took a chug of his Coors and started to turn away.

I tugged on his sleeve. "My gynecologist said I should let you know," I said. "He told me it was the only socially responsible way to handle the situation."

Josef stood and started for the door.

"I'm not paying for an abortion," he said.

I stopped in my tracks, bent from the waist and laughed. "You gave me herpes," I said. "It could have been so much worse, couldn't it? He was a man I'd just as soon forget but never would."

THE BARON'S DANCE

Paulette was only twelve when Princess Diana got married, but she and her sister, Christine had watched every moment of the wedding, wrapped in quilts and snuggling on the couch. They'd done the same for the funeral those too few years later, though Christine had to drive in from Cleveland where she now lived with her husband and new baby daughter. The agony and the ecstasy, that was life. Today was Paulette's ecstasy. She was marrying the man of her dreams. By nightfall she'd be Mrs. John William Sutter. She'd be married to a man she trusted, loved and respected. A man whose goal in life from the day he met her had been to take care of her. John had some shadows in his life; parts that Paulette didn't understand or couldn't quite see but time would take care of that. And there was the money, plenty of it and lots of time to spend it thanks to Sutter Automotive - Cars for Sale. That was John's family business. It meant John dealt with an occasional unsavory type, with garlic breath or greasy sideburns who made Paulette's skin crawl, but John said it was part of any business dealing with the public. "The public just isn't what it used to be," John said and laughed when Paulette asked him. He handled them with aplomb and strength. John was no thin-lipped, big-eared wimp like Diana's prince.

"Trust is the most important thing," Christine said. The sisters were sharing a wedding breakfast for two in Paulette's suite. Christine sipped her mimosa.

"More important than love?" Paulette said. "I thought it was love that conquered all."

"Love's important, but trust, that's what gets me through." Christine said. "I have to know my husband will be there when I need him and if he isn't there, he'll come fast as he can the moment I call."

Paulette toyed with the eggs benedict. "John would leap tall buildings for me. I have no doubt." She said it fiercely.

"Good, because there are lots of tall buildings in a marriage. And never once, not once let yourself think of divorce."

"It's my wedding day, Chrissie. How can you even say the word?"

"Do you think Diana thought of divorce before she married Charles? Ivana before she married Donald? It happens, Pauley. Don't let it happen to you."

"Have you ever thought of divorcing Clinton?"

Chrissie filled her champagne flute from the pitcher on the table, took a sip. "No," she said.

Paulette studied herself in the mirror while Chrissie and the bridesmaids twittered around her and the photographer snapped candid shots. She was a bride, a beautiful bride, dressed in white. It suited her. It was worth the trouble and the self-denial to be a bride dressed in white on your wedding day. Today was hers; she wanted to savor every second. She wanted to remember this day to her grave.

Her mother hugged her and tucked a hanky of palest blue lace into her bouquet. "I carried this the day I married your father," she said. "Chrissie carried it when she married Clinton. Today, it's yours."

Chrissie adjusted her veil, "You look perfectly beautiful. We'll all be lucky if John doesn't faint dead away at the sight of you."

They could hear the swell of The Wedding March coming from the sanctuary. Paulette's father took her arm. "I've been the best father I knew how. I'm sure John will be the best husband."

Paulette hugged her father's arm, tears dampened his eyes and together they walked down the aisle where John waited at the altar: tall, strong, incredibly handsome, and smiling just for her.

"It's time for us to go," John whispered in Paulette's ear. His arms were around her possessively as they danced. He was aroused and Paulette was slightly drunk from champagne.

"Yes," Paulette said. Her breath was warm and sweet against his cheek.

They said goodnight to Paulette's parents, thanked them for the wedding and hurried upstairs to their suite. John swiped his key card through the lock and pushed open the door. He swooped Paulette into his arms and carried her over the thresh hold. The air was heavy with the sweet scent of lilies. Heavy, cloying, enough to make Paulette's stomach lurch. John's lips were on her neck, kissing, caressing, eager to carry her away. John pushed the door shut with his foot and kissed Paulette deeply before he set her feet back on the floor.

"My wife," John said. "My beautiful wife forever." He kissed her again pressing tight against her so she could feel his erection through the silk of her gown.

"I am yours," Paulette said.

"Not just yet," a third voice said and four men stepped into the room. The fat man held a gun pointed at Paulette. She had seen two of them before at Sutter Automotive.

Paulette looked to John, but he had already been grabbed by two of the men and the third had slapped a length of duct tape across his mouth.

It happened so fast.

"What...?" Paulette said and was cut off by the fat man.

"Shut up," he said and Paulette did.

She watched as one man drug a straight backed chair from the corner and John was taped into it, arms piniomed at his sides, feet crossed at the ankles. He struggled against the three, his eyes bulged with anger as he kicked and fought and finally was subdued. Through it all Paulette stood like a pillar of salt, aware of the smell of lilies and with the heat of terrified blood racing through her veins.

"We've come to take our cut," the fat man said, "right off the top." His phlegmy chuckle filled the room. "We're partners, right? Share and share alike." And two of the others grabbed Paulette by the arms as she turned to run towards the door, as she opened her mouth to scream. The third slapped a length of duct tape over her nose and mouth.

"Promise you'll be quiet?" the fat man said.

Paulette struggled, tried to free her arms. She shook her head in rage.

"I'll give you a minute to consider," the fat man said. "For your own sake, think fast."

She had no air, her knees were weak and her white silk gown was drenched in frightened sweat.

John rattled the chair against the floor trying to break free. Paulette begged with her eyes.

"Okay, she's had enough, Spider. Take off the tape," the fat man said.

Spider was a skinny man, all arms and legs. He jerked the tape off and Paulette gasped in the lily scented air. Grateful, breathing, alive. Tears filled her eyes, an angry red rectangle marked her face where the tape had been.

"Don't think of this as rape," the fat man said. "Think of it as the Baron's Dance."

"Yeah, like in the movie Braveheart," Spider said. "The landowner gets the first piece of every bride on his property." He was leering now.

"Except I want Johnny here to see every move," the fat man said. "I never want him to forget who has the power." He walked to John and slapped him across the face. "Pay attention, Johnny."

John struggled against the tape, tipping the chair with the force of his anger, or perhaps it was fear. "Set him back up," the fat man said and the other men did.

Paulette buried her face in her hands and the three men began to circle. Her throat tightened and the breath stuck there.

"You goin' first?" Spider asked the fat man.

He looked at Paulette for a long minute. "No, she's not my type."

Spider grabbed his crotch. "I got some power for her," he said. "Can I go first?"

The other men laughed and the fat man nodded. He said, "Pay attention, Johnny."

Paulette screamed but a fresh piece of tape was slapped across her mouth before it ended.

Her nightmare began and her dreams died as each of the three men had her. On the couch, on the floor, bent across a table. Her white silk gown was a tattered rag, tossed aside as they forced her, and forced her and forced her. The fat man kept the gun pointed at John through it all.

"I think she liked it," Spider said. Paulette was rolled into a fetal ball on the floor. Her breasts were bruised and her hair fell in tangles. She could smell the sharpness of her own sweat, mixed with the lily smell and the odor the men left on her. She fought against throwing up behind the tape.

"I own you, Johnny Sutter and now I own her too. Don't you forget it."

The men left the suite.

Paulette sobbed.

John rocked the straight-backed chair till it tipped again and clattered over sideways.

Finally Paulette looked at him; pure shame filled her eyes. She picked up the tangled bridal gown and held it to her, head hanging forward, hair covering her face.

John rocked the chair against the floor and when she looked at him, he motioned with his eyes and she went to him, walking carefully against the pain. Sweat poured from his brow and anger filled his eyes. Paulette tried to right the chair. John shook his head, aimed his eyes downward trying to get her to understand. The tape, the tape.

She knelt beside him and took an edge of tape and tried to lift it. Tape and skin pulled against one another. John jerked his head back and the tape pulled loose from Paulette's fingers. She tried again and this time pulled the tape loose with a hard, fast motion that also pulled off skin.

"Jesus," John said. "That hurt."

Paulette sat back on her heels the white silk still clutched against her bosom. Her eyes were blank, staring into nowhere.

"Paulette," John yelled, "Find a knife, cut me loose."

Moving woodenly, Paulette did. Then she collapsed onto the couch.

John freed himself and stomped the room.

"Dirty, fat bastard," he yelled. He kicked the chair into the wall. Tape still hung from its bottom rungs.

"John, who were those men?" Paulette asked. "Why has this happened?"

"It's business, Paulette. It has nothing to do with you."

Her eyes darkened and she looked at John. "It had something to do with me, John. At least it does now." She stood and dropped the silken rags, exposing her body. Finger-shaped bruises laced her arms where the men had held her down, where they had pinched her and bitten her.

"Are you hurt?" John said. "Do you need to see a doctor?"

"I've been raped by three men, John. Of course I'm hurt."

John sat beside her on the couch. He put an arm around her bare shoulders and pulled her to him. She jerked herself free.

"What goes on at Sutter Automotive? Drugs? Gambling? Murder? What is it?"

"We sell cars."

"And more?"

John hesitated before he spoke. "It's the money. The money is what makes it matter and I've been trying to break free. I wanted to be on my own."

Paulette didn't say a word. She just looked at John Sutter, her husband.

"I wanted it for us," John said. "For you and me but it will have to wait. This changes everything. I can't put you at risk again?"

"I've just been raped."

"It was the Baron's Dance, Paulette, an old custom, a ritual from history. Think of it that way."

He ran a hand through his hair and stood. "I'll run you a hot bath. You can soak. We can't get the police involved in this."

"It is my wedding night," Paulette said. Her voice was flat, the smell of lilies still hung in the air.

"My wife," John said. "My beautiful wife, forever."

Paulette could only think of a black BMW, crumpled and broken, with a princess bleeding in the back seat.

THE LIBERATION OF CARMEN CARTER

Life on the street is hard, even when you're young. Carmen Carter was no longer young. She was thirty-eight and had been on the street twenty years. They were a lot like dog years and she had aged seven for every year she'd spent walking the block between Main and High, turning most of her earnings over to Armand at the end of every shift.

"Strictly Business," Armand said after one particularly long night. Carmen had done drunken frat boys, the entire pledge class from Delta Upsilon Alpha, and a group of 4-Hers in from Lima. Nobody had a gold card and everybody wanted to go "Around the world." Carmen liked the regulars better. The men who depended on a whore and weren't just doing it on a dare. Some days were better than others.

"Easy for you," Carmen said. "I'm the one who has to lead their asses up three flights of stairs and then collect the money. One of the 4-H'ers paid with rolls of coins."

"Quarters or pennies," Armand asked.

Carmen pulled two rolls of quarters from the pocket of her short leather jacket and laid them on the table.

"It could have been worse," Armand said.

"Twenty dollars...for around the world." Carmen sighed. "I used to get that just to have a drink."

"Neither of us is getting any younger," Armand said.

Carmen pulled wads of wrinkled bills from her pockets. "Whew," she said. "Even their money smells like stale beer. I hate the young ones."

"They're fast," Armand said. "Slam, bam, thank you ma'am. When the price goes down, the volume has to go up. It's simple economics." He separated the bills into piles of ones, fives, tens and twenties on the table. Tipped his chair back on two legs and eyed Carmen from beneath thick black brows.

"Only $520," he said.

"Do you have any idea what it's like to go around the world twenty-six times in eight hours?" Carmen pulled off a stiletto-heeled shoe, cocked one leg against the other and massaged her foot.

"You're working on your back. How hard can it be?"

Carmen sighed. "I really wish you'd take on another girl," she said. "I need a break." She put her shoe back on, rubbed her jaw and grimaced. "Besides I've got a toothache that won't quit. I think I need to see a dentist."

Armand pulled out his ledger book and recorded the totals for the day. His face had a worried look. Then he got up and offered Carmen his chair. She sat gingerly on one hip. He rubbed her shoulders and she relaxed a bit as his fingers and thumbs dug out the tension.

Armand carefully divided the money into two piles and gave Carmen her share of the nights earnings. "It will cut into the monthly bottom line," he said, "but take tomorrow off. Get a good night's sleep. See the dentist. Nobody wants a toothless whore."

"Advanced gingivitis," Dr. Zimmerman said. She was young and cute and the third dentist Carmen called. Her practice was new and she was able to work her in. She shook her head and a frown creased her forehead, "I'm afraid they are going to have to come out."

"A tooth is going to have to come out?" Carmen asked with a cringe. "Which one?"

"All of them." She held an x-ray up to the light. "You have deep, deep cavities in four. The enamel on your teeth is worn and nearly gone. Almost like the teeth of a bulimic whose been throwing up for years." She shook her head. "You're not one of those are you?"

"No," Carmen said.

"It's the stomach acid coming up," she said. "After a while it almost dissolves the teeth." She was wearing green scrubs like a hospital orderly. She hitched them up. Carmen wished she could get away with a work wardrobe like that.

"How about caps?" Carmen asked.

"I don't think so," the dentist said. She studied the x-rays some more. "Your bone is deteriorated and caps might work for a while - a year or so - but eventually these teeth are going to have to come out."

Carmen could tell from the tilt of the dentist's head, she'd reached her final answer.

"I don't have insurance," Carmen said. "How much will all this cost?"

"$5,750.00," the dentist said, "in advance." She didn't crack a smile.

Carmen did a quick calculation in her head, That was 288 trips around the world, if she could get Armand to forego his cut. She sighed. "I'll have to think about it," she said.

"You knew there was no dental insurance when you signed on," Armand said.

He was studying the ledger book. "There have been other fringe benefits. A trip to Cancun in 1998, a Christmas bonus in 1996 . . ." He thumbed through the ledger looking for proof of his generosity.

"I was eighteen years old when I signed on and I didn't know shit. Carlos paid for the trip to Cancun so he didn't have to risk foreign whores, and the Christmas bonus was a lousy $100."

"How about workman's comp?"

"Can we prove it's a job-related injury?"

Armand was quiet.

"I didn't think so. Besides, you have to pay into the system for me to take out of the system."

"I suppose you're going to tell me now you didn't know we were operating outside the system all these years."

Carmen paced, getting more agitated by the minute. "I've been arrested forty-two times. I'm not going to claim what I'm doing is as legal as taking dictation. But I am going to need some financial help and I'll have to take a few days off."

Armand's shoulders slumped like they were carrying the weight of the world. "Maybe I should take on another girl. How about the dentist? She's already experienced at working with bodily orifices."

"She's getting over $5000 a crack. This would be quite a comedown for her."

"It could be a unique marketing tool," Armand said. "One thing would take your mind off the other."

Carmen gave him a look of complete disgust.

"I guess you're right," Armand said. He closed the ledger and laid it to one side.

"Get a young one," Carmen said, "who isn't tired and in need of repair."

Armand nodded. "I could use some young stuff myself. I'll check out the bus station and the runaway homes this afternoon."

"How about the money?" Carmen said.

Armand pursed his lips. "I could spot you a thousand," he said. "I've got an investment to protect."

"I'll take it."

A month later, Carmen was flat on her back, her jaw and gums dead to this world, her mouth spread open wide like it was waiting for Long Dong Silver or something. Dr. Zimmerman was humming softly and rocking back and forth, one by one loosening Carmen's bottom teeth with an instrument she had discretely kept hidden till she plunged it into Carmen's mouth. Carmen appreciated the fact that she hadn't been expected to admire the instrument before it did its dirty work.

"Do you enjoy your work," Carmen asked when there was a break in the action. Her lower lip and tongue weren't working properly so it came out, "Ew u enoy ur erk?"

"I love the people," the doc said. "Dentistry is a good profession, but I do have the worry of $95,000 in student loans." A frown creased Dr. Zimmerman's forehead as she stuck her tool back in Carmen's mouth and began rocking another tooth loose from the sickly gum tissue.

Carmen couldn't compute in her head how many trips around the world that calculated out to.

Pulling teeth was hard work. It took some physical strength and small beads of perspiration formed on the dentist's upper lip as she progressed. She sang and she rocked and one by one she extracted Carmen's teeth.

"What line of work are you in?" the dentist asked when she took another break.

Carmen gulped blood and saliva that hadn't been aspirated by the assistant. "I'm a whore," she said. "With false teeth will I still be able to..."she hesitated wanting to put it delicately.

Dr. Zimmerman's eyes lit up. "Double your prices. You are going to be a sought after commodity with no teeth."

Carmen wanted to curve her lips into a smile, but with all the Novacain in them, she couldn't do it. Just like Gypsy Rose Lee she was going to have a gimmick. Or as Armand would say: a wonderful marketing tool.

When Carmen returned home, Armand had the new girl with him. Her name was Ashley. She was fourteen-years-old and had just turned her first trick.

"I'm not used to condoms," she said in a petulant tone.

"The first rule of the street," Armand said, "is the John has to wear a condom. I can't afford to lose my investment by having you get sick after I've spent time and money training you." Armand was pouring over the ledger book and finally recorded a zero for the day. "The entire first quarter is turning into a disaster."

"It wasn't my fault," Ashley said. "The minute I touched him, it was over."

"It's better to go for the old guys in the beginning," Carmen said. Her lips and tongue were moving better but the pain was escalating as the Novocain wore off. The dentist had put her new teeth into her mouth as soon as the extractions were finished. "To prevent swelling," she said. They felt huge to Carmen, like she had a truck in her mouth. "At least till you perfect your technique."

"The condoms are a must," Armand said. He threw a handful of foil wrapped packs on the table in front of Ashley, went to the refrigerator and pulled out a large kielbasa sausage. He lay it on the table. "Practice till you can do it with your eyes closed."

"Gross," the girl said but she unwrapped a condom and fumbled with it till it began to unroll over the sausage. It was crooked and before she was finished she'd poked a hole in it with her thumb.

"Employee training is a real expense," Armand said.

"Practice," Carmen said, "and technique. Let me show you." She took one of the foil packs and using just one hand tore it open. She applied it to the sausage and in one motion had the sausage perfectly sheathed.

The girl tried again with Armand and Carmen watching. Again she bungled the job. "Do it a hundred times," Armand said, "Try to use each condom at least three times." Carmen gave him a disgusted look. "You can't reuse a condom," she said.

"This is just like school," Ashley said. "And my parents' fighting. Those are the reasons I ran away." Using her arm as a broom she swiped the table clean. The sausage and foil packs littered the floor. "I'm out of here." And she stomped out of the room without a backward look.

"Recruiting is a little harder than I expected," Armand said. He gathered the condoms up off the floor and stuck the sausage back into the refrigerator. "I talked to a dozen girls before I convinced this one to give it a try." He shook his head sadly. "And she forgot to collect the money."

"No sense of values," Carmen said. "What was she charging?'

"Fifty dollars for a hand job and up the scale from there."

"And she got that?"

"No. She didn't get anything. I told you she forgot to collect." Armand's chin drooped and pulled his face into a look of profound sadness.

Carmen rubbed her mouth. It hurt like hell. "I have to rest a while," she said, "and it will take at least three days for my gums to heal."

Armand muttered to himself about sagging profits and first quarter earnings as Carmen left the room.

Armand paraded a dozen potential new girls through his screening program and all them had a fatal flaw of some kind.

~ 127 ~

"You've got to get back on the street," he said to Carmen when she dropped in on the afternoon of the third day.

"I'm reporting for work," she said. "These teeth hurt like I have a dozen tiny blades at work in my mouth, but I'm reporting for work. I need the money, too."

Armand smiled. "Thank God for the older generation."

It was a warm night and foot traffic was heavy on the street. It was a hooker's paradise. Carmen's first trick was a regular, a Republican politician whose Republican wife and all his girlfriends were adverse to oral sex. He didn't have an intern.

"How they hanging, Marcus?" Carmen said with some familiarity when they got to her room.

"Tight," he said. "Tight and in desperate need of your services."

"You want the usual, then?"

"Yeah," he said as he unbuckled his pants and let them slide to the floor. Carmen assumed a prayerful position in front of him and began her work. The new teeth bobbed around in her mouth, cutting into her gums like twenty tiny saw blades.

"Something's not right," Marcus said, his hand clutching a handful of her bright red hair.

Carmen sighed and leaned back, "I was afraid of this," she said. She bowed her head and slipped the new teeth from her mouth, tucked them into the pocket of her leopard print shorts, and bent back to her task. A blow job had never been so easy...or so smooth . . or so fast. Before she looked up, Carmen wedged the new teeth back into her mouth. She grimaced at the pain.

Marcus was wobbly-kneed and dreamy-eyed as he rearranged himself and zippered up. "That was the best ever," he said. He pulled out his wallet and lay a twenty across Carmen's out stretched palm. She looked deep into his eyes and didn't close her hand around the bill. He pulled out another one and added it to the first. "You're right," he said. "and don't think I won't spread the word. You are moving up in the world, my girl."

Carmen smiled, showing her brand new teeth, and silently thanked the wise and wonderful dentist who had helped her find the way to make her fortune.

THE BEZEL BOX

The March wind was cold and gusty as Harry and I performed our last service to our mother by throwing her ashes into Lake Erie. The wind blew some of the ashes back into our faces. I could taste the gritty residue. Ashy flecks clung to my brother's hair just above his ear. It would have been kind of me to reach over and brush them loose, but we had never been close.

It had been a week from Hell since my Aunt Hildy called saying Mother had fallen, hit her head and recovery was unlikely. "A brain stem injury," she said. "She hasn't regained consciousness. The doctors say she probably won't."

I wasn't completely surprised. She was eighty-six and during the past year had begun to look old and frail. But still she was my mother and I wasn't prepared for death's final separation. It had come anyway and after the service we had received condolences from an amazing number of her friends in the church parlor. She had touched a lot of people besides my brother and me. Her life and been long and full. There was a certain satisfaction in that.

Harry and I walked away from the cliff that rimmed the lake, joined our women waiting in separate cars and returned to our mother's empty house. The last time we were in the house together was when our father died ten years ago. We both came ahead of our families-of-the-moment to help our mother with the arrangements.

"It feels so good to have you here together, again," she said. Tears filled her eyes.

"I'm sure it does," Harry said. He patted her narrow shoulder.

"We've got to do it more often," she said looking from one of us to the other.

I nodded agreement but Harry and I both knew our separate visits were by design and grew from circumstances we couldn't change or let go. We even lived in separate states now and we both knew today would probably be our last time together now that our parents were both gone. It was the day to settle things between us. It was the last chance for both of us to find some resolution to the things that divided us . . . or not. We didn't speak of this but set about doing what we had agreed to do. Take the things we wanted from our family home and leave everything else for the liquidators to turn into cash. The women went into the kitchen to make tea and Harry and I began our task in the living room.

"I want the Bezel Box," I said running a finger over its brass scrollwork.

The box sat on my mother's desk where it had been as long as I can remember. My grandfather brought it home from the Spanish American War in 1904, a personal gift to him from the Sultan of Sulu. It is bronze colored, the size of a loaf of bread and covered with intricate metal coils hand rolled by the Sulu natives. It has a lid that opens like a coffin and is remarkably heavy for its size.

"I want it, too," Harry said. He scowled from under bushy brows that brought our father to my mind. "You can have the phonograph equipment and the encyclopedia."

I wondered if he was serious. The phonograph was a 1950 vintage high fidelity set and the encyclopedia was a Compton's 1958 edition, bought to help me with my homework back in junior high school. Harry never needed any help with his. I considered walking out of the room but didn't want to leave him alone to pack the Bezel Box into the carton with his name across the side so I said, "I don't want them. The liquidators can sell them. I want the Bezel Box."

"Mom always left surprises for me in that box. It's special to me," he said.

"For US, Harry. She left surprises for US in that box." It had been candy and gum when we were small boys, money when we reached school age and cartoons, inspirational poems and thoughts on life when we became men. In the early years, my brother had a habit of cleaning out the box and leaving it empty for me. It was empty again today.

Harry leaned back in his chair, a self-satisfied smile on his face. He knew he'd gotten to me. I felt twelve years old again and second-best to Harry. I was angry the years and distance had changed so little between us, perhaps had changed so little about me.

"The box is a link between grandfather and me, too." Harry said. "I AM named after him and DID serve in the military, like he did. I should have his war trophy." He laced his fingers together across his chest and leaned forward in the chair. "It's a bonified heirloom and I'm the eldest son. By rights, I should have it."

"Mother's will says share and share alike, all the worldly goods between my beloved sons. She gave no advantage to the eldest." I lifted the box in both hands. It was too heavy to do otherwise.

"Sharing," Harry said and leaned back into the chair, wiggled the bushy brows. "Yes, sharing can be good.

His message was not subtle and he intended to coax blood from old wounds. Sharon was my first wife, not really up to Harry's standards, but plenty good enough for me.

Harry even got to her first and delighted in letting me know _after_ the wedding. Harry moved on to other women and so did I eventually. He'd had four wives, each one beautiful and cool.

I am re-married now, Harry is engaged. His fiancé is beautiful, my wife is not. Both women sat in the kitchen sipping tea while we negotiated. I refused to give up the Bezel Box. Harry's eyes showed anger, but I refused and he got the china and the silver. I wrapped the box in newspaper and tucked it carefully into one of the cartons my wife carried in from the Kroger store. He packed the dinnerware into boxes he'd purchased from a moving company for the occasion.

"Jessie," he called casually into the kitchen. "Come and see which of mother's knickknacks you'd like to have." She was smiling as she came into the dining room. Her eyes were cool and blue, they met mine. It would be harder to argue with her. She was still in her thirties. Harry was fifty=four on his last birthday. He touched piece after piece and she nodded her head almost imperceptibly. The items she chose went into Harry's cartons.

My wife followed me into the living room where I claimed the lamps, which I have never liked and told her to wrap the horse brass framing the windows and put them in my carton. She worked quickly, eager to please me and I was grateful for her plainness.

And so the afternoon of the day of our mother's funeral went as Harry and I separately, politely and, for the most part silently, vied for the spoils of our mother's life; our past. We were sifting jealousies, grudges and memories more dated than the encyclopedias. We agreed finally that we had enough and what was left would be turned over to the professionals for the sale. We loaded our cars with boxes, locked the doors of our mother's house and parted with a handshake in the driveway, saying vague words about staying in touch.

It was a long drive home. My wife chattered about the day. "Jessie is beautiful, isn't she?"

"If you like leggy blondes," I said.

"And youth." She said it with a smile on her lips and a question in her eye. I knew better than to respond.

"You and Harry have never gotten along?"

"We've never been close."

"He seems nice enough to me," she said. "A little competitive maybe, a little condescending to his baby brother, but nice just the same." She didn't know about Harry and my first wife. She didn't know so much and had only met Harry one other time. I figured knowing Harry would only change her opinion of me. I didn't care what she thought of Harry. I concentrated on my driving.

"I found some papers," she said. "I slipped them in an envelope and brought them with me." She smiled, satisfied with herself. "There's an odd sort of intimacy involved in going through someone's things. I feel like I know your mother better than I ever did when she was alive."

"Her attorney already has the important papers. What did you find?"

"Letters, newspaper clippings." She paused. "I threw away some things. A folder full of programs for her friends' funeral services and clippings and advice for overcoming loneliness."

"Really?" I said. "I never thought my mother was lonely. Did you?"

There was silence while she thought about her answer. "No, I never did," she said. "But I do now."

She was tired, a little sad, though it wasn't her mother who had died. I felt unreasonably irritated with her and drove faster than she liked.

"Please slow down," she said then stared silently out the window.

"Sure," I said, but didn't lift my foot from the gas pedal.

When we got home I carried in just the carton that contained the Bezel Box. I dug out the box and unwrapped it. I lifted the heavy lid and my eyes filled with tears when I saw that it was still empty. My wife laid a hand on my shoulder and pulled a white envelope from her purse. "Maybe these should go inside," she said.

In the envelope were letters in my mother's firm young handwriting. One was written the day after her wedding and told my Aunt Hildy of her joy at marrying my father. Another written the day I was born. It described the perfect beauty of her second son.

There was a crisp, yellow news clipping of my grandfather's return from the Spanish American War. In the photo he was shiny-cheeked and very young. And there was a letter from Harry, angry words describing his emptiness, his sadness at the mess he'd made of his life, even a mention of sexual dysfunction that he couldn't overcome. I read it twice, thought of sending it to Harry so he'd know I'd seen it. I shook my head and decided even Harry didn't deserve that.

I slipped the papers back into the envelope and put them into my Bezel Box, set the box on my desk and knew that my mother had filled it for the last time.

VESPERS: A PRAYER AT TWILIGHT

In the eyes of my mother's dying, I see the richness of her gift of life to me. A gift given without joy or pleasure. But my gift just the same. Mine to enjoy or squander. Mine alone.

Today my brother and I put her in a nursing home. It is the twilight of her life.

Her eyes are bright blue, sparkling and alert. They remind me of a startled predator caught in the light while at his dirty business. Her eyes are still her best feature and the only remaining object of a fierce vanity that ruled her life. All other signs of beauty are gone.

There is an unbroken stream of helpers and aides in and out of the room while my mother and I both try to get the lay of this place, maybe the final place she will live. I wonder if they will return after I leave. I see fear in the sparkle of my mother's eyes. Fear of what, I am not sure. Yet another new place? Being left alone? The inhuman noise from the other patients (the workers call them residents) wailing up the halls? Death himself? I wonder what she sees in mine.

My brother and I have chosen the best place we could find after several days of parading half-dead halls with bodies (they seem nothing more) slumped in wheelchairs parked along the walls. Smells that water the eyes and pierce the nose. Grayed heads bobbling or inert, all of them hung at unintended angles. We share a moment of mutual prayer, "Please God, hit me with a truck.", then smile nervously to cover up our truth.

Once the choice has been made we avoid one another for several days, like a band of outlaws who have split up to muddy their trail. To confound the law, escape the consequences. I believe my mother is here as a result of modern science that promotes survival, but not recovery from life's accidents. The blood clot running wild, the collapsed arteries in vital spots, the mutated cells that can be slowed, but not quite stopped. The price of "Progress" and "Increased Longevity". Products worthy of P. T. Barnum and easily salable to gullible consumers. I do not know what my brother thinks.

Finally, all the papers have been signed, all the putting off has been done and I have to leave her there. A pleading look fills her eyes. Tears threaten mine, but I turn and walk out of her room, negotiate the halls making no contact with the residents parked along the way, till I make it through to the door and outside into the good fresh air which I gulp and savor. "Please God, give me strength," I pray.

My father died thirteen years ago, at a BP station in Lone Tree, Florida waiting to gas up the 1973 gold Cadillac he used to pull his Airstream. "Dead before he hit the ground," the sheriff said later when my brother went to collect his things. They'd been wintering in Florida since he retired (my dad's version of the American Dream) and she had flown home to save herself the discomfort of the long road trip. Most of my mother's life was lived to save herself, but it hasn't worked. "I never loved him anyway," she said when my brother told her. It rippled the pond of family life and the waves kept on coming in the fire-shower of her widowhood.

She wore a green silk suit to his funeral and while her eyes sparkled, she never cried. She began right there, in front of the grandchildren and the preacher, to size up the men who might be a part of her future. She took full advantage of being center stage.

The family was gathered around the Thanksgiving table when she announced, "I had my first orgasm last month."

My brother nearly choked on his mashed potatoes.

The teenage grandchildren blushed red and snickered behind their hands.

There'd already been a string of men (gray, smiling, hat in hand) and she told us, "I'm happy for the first time in my life." But happiness (or sensitivity) was never my mother's forte and this soon changed. Three men died and one went back to his wife.

"Who's going to take care of me now?" she asked and though my brother and I tried, she soon moved to Florida full-time where her sister and husband built on a room for her. She didn't write, she didn't call, she didn't return for holidays, but made a two week visit in the summer for any who cared to see her.

"Thank you, Lord, for small blessings," I said.

It was the seventies. My husband left me with three small children for a twenty-year-old who could suck the chrome off a trailer hitch.

"You've made your bed, now you have to lie in it," my mother said.

"I knew you'd never be able to keep a man spouting that woman's lib stuff," my father said.

From my parents I got neither comfort, nor cash. It was a bleak time for me and my mother said. "This is for your own good. Learn to stand alone."

I smiled, got a job, dropped out of organized religion, took care of my children and eventually married again.

"Please God, don't let me fail again," I prayed.

I was twelve the first time I realized my mother didn't love me. It was summer. Hot and I'd failed to satisfy some wish of hers. Her eyes were snapping with anger, perspiration beaded on her lip. "I tried to get an abortion when I knew I was pregnant with you. We'd have all been better off."

I made no response but cried myself to sleep that night. My brother heard the noise and came into my room. He laid a hand on my shoulder, said, "Are you okay?" I lied and said I was just crying over a sad movie I had seen. I spent the next ten years trying to prove that I was worthy of being on this earth. Good grades, hard work, responsible behavior. Nothing worked and I pretended to forget, but I didn't.

"Please God, let somebody love me," I begged.

I was born and life is large and grand. My mother gave me life and I wish I could do the same for her. But I can't.

"Please God, let me live mine better." Amen.

OTHER BOOKS BY DIANA HANNON FORRESTER

Glory
Where have all the Flowers Gone?
All the World's a Stage
The Old Lady Book

With Jan Biggs and Mary Clark
Writing as Alma Lynn Thompson

The Guild in the Granary
Timeless Star
Double Wedding Ring

For more great stories please visit our website:

www.BadgleyPublishingCompany.com

www.ingramcontent.com/pod-product-compliance
Lightning Source LLC
Chambersburg PA
CBHW071957170626
46813CB00005B/1914